This book is dedicated to Kaitlyn Nicole Fabry, who is—and forever will be—our Kaity Belle.

Checkered Flag
CHRIS FABRY
DISCARD

TYNDALE HOUSE PUBLISHERS, INC., CAROL STREAM, ILLINOIS

"I think a learning driver is a winning driver."

Dale Earnhardt

"Boogity, boogity, boogity! Let's go racing, boys."

Darrell Waltrip

"To finish first you must first finish."

Rick Mears

"Success is being happy with yourself."

Kyle Petty

"The good Lord doesn't tell you what his plan is, so all you can do is get up in the morning and see what happens next."

Richard Petty

Chapter 1
Denver

JAMIE MAXWELL STARED at the scoring pylon, and her jaw dropped. The second car to qualify was passing the start/finish line—engine screaming. Her thoughts clouded as she stared at the Rocky Mountains against a clear blue sky in the distance and tried to recall the track record. She had run the simulator at the experimental school many times, but the numbers jumbled in her head. She thought she remembered the record, but her time was almost a second faster.

"That can't be right," she muttered, unbelieving. "What's the track record here?"

T.J. Kelly, her dad's crew chief, smiled. "You blew it away in the first lap and went faster in the second. Your dad's gonna jump out of his skin when he hears this."

The second car's time wasn't even close to Jamie's. "I knew we had a good car, but to get under the track record . . ."

Crew members ran over to her, and it was obvious they expected to see Dale getting out of the car. When they saw it was Jamie, they looked at the scoring pylon and then at her.

Scotty, the Maxwell spotter, patted Jamie on the back. "Good job."

"Think it'll hold up?" she said.

The third car had passed the start/finish line and the speed flashed.

Scotty shook his head. "I wouldn't be surprised if it held up today and all the way to the next time you qualify here." He winked at her.

A camera crew hurried over, and a reporter shoved a microphone in Jamie's face. He shouted a question over the engine noise on the track, something about her dad not being there. Jamie could barely hear him, but her training at the school came back. It didn't really matter what the question was—they wanted something fresh and with emotion.

"My dad got hung up, and he asked me to qualify for him. I just put my foot down and went as fast as I could."

"What's it feel . . . broke track record?" the guy said, his voice going in and out with the noise.

"This track hasn't been here that long," Jamie said. "And my dad says that records are made to be broken. I just hope he gets a good starting position."

Jamie noticed Butch Devalon's crew chief talking with one of the officials, pointing toward her and shouting.

The reporter asked her something else, and she asked him to repeat it. "How long before you're out here taking over for your dad?" the reporter said.

Jamie laughed. "You don't know my dad. They'll have to use a crowbar to get him out of that #14 car. I want to do anything I can to help him get into the Chase."

"Well, it's clear you've given him a good chance at that," the reporter said.

Jamie followed T.J. back to the hauler, getting pats on the back from crew members of other teams. A bunch of them shook their heads and chuckled as she walked past as if they'd never seen a female go that fast.

Back at the hauler, T.J. shut the door and turned to her. "How'd it feel?"

Jamie couldn't hold it in anymore. She pumped her fist in the air and shouted, "That was the best thing that's ever happened to me! It was like I was part of the car and there wasn't anything holding me back and . . ." She continued for another minute, trying to explain.

T.J.'s cell phone rang, and he handed it to her. "You talk to him."

"Dad, did you hear?" Jamie said.

Her dad's voice was strained, and she guessed it was from the stress of being snookered by Butch Devalon. "I called home, and your mom watched the whole thing on SPEED. You really know how to get her to pray."

"It was great out there."

"Well, you can thank Butch Devalon for this. And it looks like you can thank him for stirring up a hornet's nest about your age."

"What?"

"They've filed a protest about you even being out there on the track."

"Already? This was a setup. They knew you wouldn't be able to qualify since they took you away."

"I know. Don't worry. I don't think it'll stand up. Besides, now they have to contend with people who'll say they're afraid of racing against a girl. You have a license, and it's the track's choice about whether to let you on it or not. They did. That settles it."

When Jamie's dad reached the track, a mob of reporters met him at the front gate. Jamie watched the coverage on the hauler TV. Her dad could have driven straight through the crowd, but he got out, which told her he wanted to talk.

"Looks like he's enjoying himself," T.J. said.

Jamie nodded. "It's been a while since anybody's wanted to interview him other than to ask about his sponsor problems."

Her dad listened to the questions, the microphones reflecting in his sunglasses, the sun beating down. "I got some bad information about the qualifying time, so I asked my daughter to sit in for me. I hear she did a pretty good job."

"Was it Butch Devalon who gave you that bad info?" a reporter said.

"I can't blame anybody but myself," her dad said. "I'm just glad I had a backup to sit in the seat for me. And from what I've heard, it looks like I got the pole position."

"What do you think about the controversy over your daughter's age?" another reporter said.

"I'll let the officials haggle over that one, but I will say this: if all of these manly men are afraid of what a little 17-year-old girl can do on the track, they'd better get ready, because the Tigress is coming."

"I can't believe he said that," Jamie said.

"Has a ring to it," T.J. said. "Tigress Maxwell."

"So you're not going to get into the controversy?" a reporter pressed.

"She earned her license. It's legit. They let her onto the track. She outraced every car out there. I think that settles it."

"So you're saying her time ought to stand."

"I'm saying if she'd have qualified 44th or worse, whoever is making a stink about this wouldn't have a problem in the world. They would have enjoyed it. But since she's beaten them, they're concerned about the rules. Jamie accomplished something out there on the track, where it counts. Of course it should stand."

Chapter 2
Spice Cake

TIM CARHARDT GRABBED some spice cake and juice from the snack table at the front of the high school meeting room and sat in his usual place. Church kids straggled in, yawning. The guys all had bed hair, and their clothes hung on them like they were a few sizes too big. The girls were the exact opposite. Every hair in place. Perfumed up and smelling like they were in some kind of contest for who could attract the most bees. All of them in their Sunday best.

Tim's approach to church was pretty much like school—he sat in the back and tried not to attract attention. For the most part, he'd been successful. Oh, the leader of the group had said hello to him every time, using Tim's name. Pastor Gordon was his name. He looked like some guy who had stepped right out of a magazine advertisement for hair conditioner, but he seemed okay. His new wife had made an effort to welcome Tim too, but he tried to avoid them.

Cassie Strower strolled in with Mrs. Gordon, talking, laughing, and cradling her Bible to her chest. She noticed Tim and waved, moving through the plastic folding chairs toward him. She didn't eat donuts or drink juice and seemed to always carry a bottle of water.

"Isn't it great about Jamie?" she said, sitting in front of him. "Did you see the coverage yesterday or the article in the newspaper?"

Tim had heard the guy who delivered their paper pass by the driveway early this morning in a truck that sounded like it needed a new exhaust and plugs for the engine. It was still dark, but Tim couldn't get back to sleep, so he walked out to get the paper and have a look. The reporter's name was Calvin Shoverton, and he had interviewed Jamie and Dale about her qualifying run. Tim had left the paper open on the kitchen table for Mrs. Maxwell and gone for a walk. He came back with wet shoes and cuffs and smelled Mrs. Maxwell's eggs and biscuits cooking—a Sunday morning treat she'd started making him when she learned he liked them.

"Yeah, looks like old Devalon's plan backfired on him," Tim said.

Cassie nodded. "I talked with Jamie late last night, and she was as happy as I'd ever heard her. It's almost like God is rewarding her in some way. You knew about what happened to her, right?"

"I don't know what you're talking about."

Cassie talked about a "spiritual awakening" or something like that. She believed Jamie had finally committed her life to God. Cassie said she'd been praying for Jamie a long time and couldn't be more excited and blah, blah, blah. All this God junk was okay for some people, but not Tim. He just stared at her and listened until her mouth stopped moving.

"Yeah, that's great," he said, taking another bite of spice cake. Christians really got to him sometimes with their talk about changed lives and new hearts and "the Spirit" moving and stuff like that. They had a language all their own, but he had to admit they made mean spice cake.

Pastor Gordon got their attention, so Cassie turned around. They took prayer requests, and Cassie mentioned Jamie.

Pastor Gordon said, "We really need to remember her and her dad in Denver today and pray that Dale would get another opportunity to bring God glory."

Tim wiped his hands on his pants and rolled his eyes. These were good people, but what they really wanted was for Dale to win, and they wanted God on their side. Tim wanted Dale to win too, but not because of God. And if Cassie was right that Jamie had jumped off the deep end into the religious pool, then the whole family had gone over the edge. He appreciated everything Dale and Mrs. Maxwell wanted to do for him by taking him into their family, and Kellen was a fun kid to play with, but Tim was sure they wanted him to believe like them and live like them and get dressed up and go to church, which he didn't like. But what alternative did he have?

"Any other requests?" Pastor Gordon said.

Somebody's mother was having surgery, another person's cat was sick, and on and on. Tim wanted to put duct tape over their mouths so they could pray silently.

Tim closed his eyes and put his head in his hands.

Somebody nudged him, and he woke up with Cassie staring at him and other people laughing. "You were kind of snoring," Cassie whispered.

"Sorry," he said, looking at the pastor.

Pastor Gordon smiled and picked up his Bible. "So what do we see about this woman who comes to the well?"

"She was thirsty?" a guy named Trace said.

Everybody laughed.

"That's not a bad observation," Pastor Gordon

said. "And isn't it interesting that Jesus was right there when this thirsty woman came along?"

Cassie raised a hand. "Didn't people usually go to draw water when it was cool—like in the morning and evening?"

"Good point," he said. "You usually didn't see anybody there in the middle of the day because it was hot. So why would this woman have come there then?"

"Maybe she was baking spice cake," Trace said.

Everybody but Pastor Gordon laughed. He looked to the back of the room. "Tim, what do you think? Why would this woman come at the hottest part of the day to do something nobody else wanted to do at that time?"

Tim shrugged. "Probably wanted everybody to leave her alone."

The pastor smiled. "That's exactly it. Very good. As we see later in the passage, this woman had done a bunch of bad things. She had a bad reputation. So it makes sense that she would come when no one else was there."

Pastor Gordon said Jesus was there at the well, and because there was a problem between his people and her people they shouldn't have talked, but they did. She'd had a bunch of husbands, and Pastor Gordon compared her to some women who hung around NASCAR garages looking for a new boyfriend.

"Jesus knew she was sinful, but he offered her living water," Pastor Gordon said.

Tim was just as confused as the woman about the living water stuff, but he listened and tried to understand. He had never thought much of Jesus. He'd heard his name at the tracks, of course, but not in a good way. He always thought of Jesus as a guy with a halo around his head, with a blank stare and ready to jump on anybody who did anything wrong. But if this story was true and he offered something to this woman who had done a lot of bad things, maybe Tim was wrong about the guy. Maybe there was something more.

He tuned out the rest of the message, and when it was over he walked into the hall.

Cassie caught up with him. "Good observation in there. You were paying attention."

"Even a blind hog finds an acorn every now and then," Tim said, repeating a saying of his father's. He moved toward the door.

"We'll be watching the race this afternoon," Cassie said.

Chapter 3
The Pole

JAMIE TOOK the cell phone from her dad and said good-bye to her mom. Her parents prayed with each other before every race, and her dad needed all the help he could get during this one. He was on the bubble to get into the Chase, which gave the top 12 racers a chance to win the cup. Jamie had qualified the #14 car for the pole position and done something no one had ever done in NASCAR—qualify when she wasn't yet 18 years old. Though the other drivers congratulated her and gave her kudos, she knew some had complained.

"She holds a valid license," one official had said. "We could have kept her off the track, but we agreed the license trumped her age."

That was the end of it, though she could have bottled Butch Devalon's stare at her during the drivers' meeting before the race. The guy had a toothpick in his mouth, and he cracked it in two while looking at her. She wanted to make a face and hold up a sign that said, "Get Over It—You've Been Clawed by the Tigress," but she didn't. She did smirk a bit, however.

Standing in the pits behind the war wagon was an experience in Denver. Because the stands were built in much the same way as Bristol's, you got the feeling of being enclosed, like at a coliseum. A canopy stretched over the stands to block the beating sun—the same kind of look as the Denver airport.

On her first trip here, Jamie had sat with her mom and Kellen in the expensive seats. Video screens were installed on the back of each seat, and you could watch a virtual dashboard of your favorite driver, listen to radio communication, and see in-car video. Whether a fan sat there or in the cheaper seats, it was one of the best places in the country to watch a race. The stands felt right on top of the track, and the infield was sunken so all the RVs and TV trucks didn't block the view.

The lighter air in Denver affected the cars in lots of ways. There was a special setup for the carburetor so it wouldn't bog down at the 5,280-foot elevation. Jamie's dad said those high-altitude directions for baking were just as important for racing.

There was a moment of silence for some victims of

a flash flood in a Colorado canyon and then a flyover from Peterson Air Force Base in Colorado Springs. The wind picked up, and all the drivers seemed concerned about the crosswinds that were gusting up to 20 mph.

Her dad took the green flag and shot ahead with a vengeance. The announcers, writers, and fans were talking about the change in her dad's racing, and Jamie could sense his confidence rising. It seemed like old times when she was little and he was in his heyday with one of the big teams. He was consistently in the top 10 in every race back then, dueling with the big guns and making the Chase. She was in elementary school and always took autographed pictures of her dad for friends. When he went out on his own, a lot of her classmates didn't want his autograph anymore.

On lap 19, two cars tapped and spun, leading to a several-car crash in the middle of the pack, many of them the top contenders. Jamie wasn't as concerned with them. The real race was between her dad and the #17 and #33 cars. The #17 car was 12th in points, with a slim margin over #33 in 13th place. Her dad was 14th and needed to move up two spots to make the Chase.

"Looking good out there, Dale," Scotty said over the radio. "Stay low and get ready for a pit stop on the next pass."

"Where's the competition?" her dad said.

"Just stay in front. We've got a long way to go," Scotty said.

Her dad got four tires and fuel, but it wasn't the crew's best pit stop. He made it back to the track in fourth place. The #17 car was right behind him in fifth, and #33 was running in 11th place.

"Looks like #17's going to push you a little bit," Scotty said.

"Us old guys need a push every now and then," her dad said.

Jamie had gone over the standings with her dad the night before. If he won the race and the two drivers ahead of him finished sixth or lower, he was in the Chase. If he came in anywhere else, it would just depend on their point totals at the end of the race.

Jamie knew other drivers were racing conservatively, not going for the win but trying to finish high. That wasn't her dad's approach, especially in this race.

Her dad attempted to get back in the lead on the outside, but he couldn't get around a faster car. That put him behind #17 with #33 only a few cars back in the pack. When #17 moved left and took a position on the inside, her dad was left alone and fell to 15th. But as her dad had said a billion times, sometimes bad things led to good things. The race leaders bunched up, and when a tire blew on one, six cars were taken out in a plume of smoke and debris.

"Go low. Go low," Scotty said. "Watch for #22 coming down the track toward you. Come on. Come on. . . . Okay, good. Clear."

Her dad made it through the wreckage and pitted again, picking up 10 spots, but he was unable to shake the #17 and #33 cars.

"More trouble coming behind," Scotty said when the green flag flew again. "You got #13 breathing down your neck."

"I figured we'd meet up at some point," her dad said.

Jamie shook her head and turned, spotting someone in a dark jacket behind her. It was Chad Devalon.

Chapter 4
Boiling

TIM'S BLOOD BOILED as he watched Butch Devalon bump Dale going into a turn. The #14 car's rear end slid to the right, and Dale tried to correct.

"Hang on to it. Hang on!" Kellen shouted.

"Whoa!" the announcers said.

"I can't believe what I just saw," one of them said.

"Well, that's how a veteran driver will hang on to it," another said. "And you won't see a better piece of driving. To hang on at these speeds is amazing."

"No yellow flag," Tim said.

"I hope his tires hold up," Kellen said.

"I hope he lets 13 by him and spins him out," Tim said.

Kellen laughed.

Ever since Tim had seen the DVD someone had left at the garage for him—

the one showing that Butch Devalon had caused his dad's death—he had been trying to come up with a way to get back at the man. He'd been banned from the tracks because of a stink Devalon had made about Tim at Brickyard, so he knew he'd have to do something off the track. But what?

While Tim mulled over his options, Dale made his way to the back of Devalon and was drafting him. The #13 and #14 cars were in tandem with several other cars lining up behind them, pushing them faster and faster around the track.

It was lap 148—only 50 left—when Dale got to the inside of #13 on turn three and the cars behind followed him. Devalon tried to move low and get in line, but he bumped the #33 car and spun him into the infield.

The yellow flag came out, and when the smoke cleared, Devalon and #33 (as well as three other cars) were out of the race.

Tim gave a whoop, and Kellen pumped his fist in the air. Mrs. Maxwell walked into the garage rubbing her hands. People from their church had joined them, watching the race in the living room, but Tim couldn't concentrate with all those people, the food, and the small talk.

Kellen told her what had happened, and she stared at the TV. "Where's the #17 car?"

Tim studied the ticker at the top of the screen. "He's dropped back to 23rd."

Mrs. Maxwell looked like she was computing some big math problem in her head. "He's close to the Chase. If he can stay here and keep this position . . ."

With 10 laps to go, Dale was in third but the #17 car was moving up fast.

"Smoke!" Kellen said.

"There's smoke coming out of the #17 car," the announcer said. "It's not clear whether that's from a tire or—"

"It's the engine," another announcer said. "This close to the Chase and the engine goes. I guess that's racing, but it's a real shame."

Tim and Kellen danced around the garage like monkeys who had found fresh bananas.

Dale pushed his car to the end and wound up in fourth place.

"And Dale Maxwell does the improbable here today—only a month ago no one would have given him a chance at the Chase, but now he's in the 12th spot," the announcer said.

"You can bet those leaders are starting to look over their shoulders," a commentator said. "With the right car, this guy can outrace anybody on the track, and he's finally driving like we all know he can."

Tim smiled and watched the remainder of the

coverage. When Kellen left, he packed up the equipment he'd been cleaning (which he did on Sunday afternoons because there was nothing else to do while he watched) and picked up a can of fuel in a red container. He sloshed the liquid a bit and set it down, opening a phone book and running his finger past the different shops until he came to "Butch Devalon Racing."

He stared at the address and tapped his finger, finally taking the can of fuel and putting it in his locker.

Chapter 5
Chase Talk

JAMIE WAITED for her dad at the hauler, not wanting to intrude on the interviews and the clamor for his answers. The people around her congratulated her as they passed. It was clear that some fans of Butch Devalon weren't too happy, but they at least tipped their caps to her.

"Well, I owe this one to my daughter, who put me in a good position," her dad said as she watched in the hauler. He also recognized the #17 and #33 teams. "They put up a real good fight, and I know they'll be right in the thick of things the rest of the season and into next year."

Just like her dad, she thought. Always complimenting others and actually meaning it, unlike most of the guys who gave backhanded compliments like, "We just beat ourselves out there."

Her dad returned to the hauler with a

few autograph hounds hanging on. Jamie came out to meet him, and a crowd gathered around both of them.

"Is this the little lady who set the track record?" a bushy-haired man said. He wore a #33 hat and a #17 jacket. "You've got a good one here, Maxwell."

"Don't I know it," her dad said, chuckling. "Now if you'll excuse us, we have some celebrating to do."

"Hold up there, Maxwell," someone said in a gruff voice.

Jamie turned and spotted the familiar black hat of Butch Devalon. He pushed past the others, banging shoulders with some, and walked straight to her dad. His teeth were on edge, and she could see a vein in the guy's forehead pulsing.

"What goes around comes around, Maxwell," Devalon said. "You'll find yourself left hanging out to dry pretty soon if you're not careful."

"Butch," her dad said in a friendly voice, "nice of you to come over and congratulate me." He put his arm around Devalon and faced the crowd. "Butch and I go way back, folks. Back further than either of us wants to admit. It's going to be a great chase down the stretch—"

Devalon moved away from him and faced Jamie, pointing a finger at her. "You may think you pulled a fast one, missy. But you just got in more trouble than you know what to do with."

Her dad straightened and stepped between them.

Jamie moved past her dad and stood toe to toe with Devalon. "Don't threaten me or my dad. You've bullied your way around these tracks long enough. Time for somebody else to be top dog."

He wagged a finger at her again, but before he could say anything, the curly-haired guy spoke. "What's the matter, Butch? You afraid this girl's gonna beat you someday?"

"Yeah, Devalon's mad because a high schooler showed him up," someone else said, and the crowd laughed.

Devalon looked around like he was an animal in the wrong cage. He turned back to Jamie, and with more of a growl than a human voice he said, "You'll pay for your insolence, young lady. And it might be your daddy who pays the most."

Before Jamie could say anything else, her dad had an arm around her and was guiding her toward the hauler. "Thank ya'll for coming—we have to get inside out of the hot air."

Inside, her dad shut the door. T.J., the crew chief, was there, going over the race.

"Top dog?" her dad said. "What's that kind of talk? We're lucky there weren't cameras around."

"That's the only reason he said that stuff," Jamie said. "He knew there wouldn't be cameras."

Her dad and T.J. laughed. It was the best sound in the world to hear those guys laughing and not stressed out because of the race.

"Hey, Dad," Jamie said, leaning forward and whispering. "You're in the Chase. You old dog, you're in the Chase, and you're gonna be top dog before you're through."

"Keep talking like that, missy," her dad said, imitating Devalon, "and you're gonna be up there on the podium with me accepting the cup."

Chapter 6
Chatter

JAMIE COULDN'T RESIST looking at the chat rooms of different racing sites. She couldn't believe how mean some of the people on one of the most popular sites could be.

From: Chatrbox2817

To: Maxwellfan1414

You really need to face the fact that Dale Maxwell is just a used-up old guy with no prayer of winning the cup. It's a shame the officials let his daughter's time stand and he got the pole at Denver. I don't think he would have done as well at New Hampshire on Sunday if that hadn't happened. Now we have to suffer through the last nine races with a guy whose last wins came 10 years ago. His only claim to fame is that he killed a gasman at Talladega. The only way Maxwell is going to win is if his daughter gets behind the wheel and shows him how to drive again.

From: Maxwellfan1414

To: Chatrbox2817

That's just plain cruel. Dale earned his spot in the Chase, and he's already moved up a spot. When he's in the winner's circle at Homestead-Miami, maybe you'll believe. Even if he doesn't make it, he has more class in his little finger than any driver you support.

From: Devalonracingfan13131313

To: Chatrbox2817

You tell them, Chatrbox. Maxwell was racing dirty in New Hampshire, and if Butch had a little help from his teammate or a friend, he would have caught him. I hate these whiny Christians who think they have some God-given right to win so they can talk about Jesus in the winner's circle.

From: BristolDixychik

To: Maxwellfan1414

I think it's time we get a serious female contender on the track, and it looks like Jamie Maxwell is just the ticket. I know she's young and she'll need to prove herself, but I hope she gets a legitimate shot at it.

From: TalladegaAl33

To: BristolDixychik

She'd probably be doing her hair in the rear-view. No female will ever make it in NASCAR because it takes too much strength and brains. That girl may have some brains, but in the heat of the race there's no way she can stand up to the other drivers. And I'm not some woman hater—that's just the truth!

From: BristolDixychik

To: TalladegaAl33

No, you're not a woman hater. You're just stupid. If that girl can win the pole at Denver, one of the toughest venues in all of racing, and win a license as one of the top drivers in that experimental school she attended, I think she's only a couple of years away from being right up there.

Some posts were so ugly that Jamie didn't want to read them, but she couldn't stop. One message made her laugh. The next made her so mad that she'd get halfway through typing a response and stop. If she ever told them who she really was, they'd never believe it and probably give her a hard time.

Her dad always had a rule about defending himself to people in chat rooms or to columnists in the newspaper or even to other drivers. He said everybody was entitled to their own opinions, no matter how wrong they were. "I'll do my defending on the track where it counts, not with a flurry of words going back and forth through the paper or the Internet or behind the garage."

Still, Jamie had a hard time not saying something

to these people. Then she noticed someone new who had logged on to the conversation.

From: CassieMaxfan

To: TalladegaAl33

I know both Jamie and her dad, and they're not whiners. They prove what they can do on the track. Period. And as for Christians talking in the winner's circle, I think it's refreshing to hear someone giving the glory to God rather than some beer company. Don't knock it until you've tried it. :)

Jamie laughed, especially at the response of TalladegaAl33, who told CassieMaxfan to keep her religion to herself and he'd keep his Budweiser in his refrigerator—though he misspelled *refrigerator* badly.

She dialed her friend Cassie, who confirmed that it was her online. The two talked half the night about the boys they knew—Chad Devalon in particular—the kids in the youth group, teachers they liked and didn't, people Cassie was praying for (it was almost easier to list the people she *wasn't* praying for), and the upcoming races.

"I really think your dad has a good chance," Cassie said.

"He keeps saying, 'All you can do is all you can do.' I wish I could have that attitude. Seems like inside he's at peace with the whole thing. Whatever happens is okay with him."

"Doesn't surprise me," Cassie said. "Some drivers seem like they hang on until they get shoved out of the car. I think it could all end tomorrow for him, and he'd be okay with it."

The thought hit Jamie in the stomach. She'd thought of her dad as invincible—always young and driving into the sunset. But his hair was gray on the sides, and when he grew his beard out, it was silver as well. The fact was that her dad's days on the track were numbered, and as she got older and better behind the wheel, he would lose a step. She wondered if there'd ever be a day when they would both be on the track in a race together.

"What about you?" Cassie said. "What's new with the Tigress?"

Jamie laughed at the nickname and growled. "Dad got me into a Legends race at Hickory."

"But you sold your car, didn't you?"

"Yeah, but Scotty, our spotter, has one he's willing to loan us for a weekend or two, so we're going to Hickory. With Dad in the Chase, I don't want to do too much, but I think it'll be fun. It'll keep me on the track."

"Birthplace of the NASCAR stars," Cassie said. "Who knows? Next year you might be moving up—don't you think?"

"One step at a time; that's what Dad says. But I've got a good start, and with what happened in Denver, we've gotten a couple of calls from possible sponsors."

"That's excellent!" Cassie said.

"And that guy from the newspaper wants to do an in-depth."

"Calvin Shoverton? You're kidding! His column is syndicated all around the country. You're going to be famous before you know it."

"Don't make me more nervous than I already am. He wants to follow our family around for a few days, and I'm trying to bribe Kellen."

"Bribe him for what?"

"So he won't be a little doofus and say something embarrassing."

"Good luck."

Chapter 7
Calvin

TIM STAYED OUT of the way of the writer guy. He couldn't believe anybody made a living sitting at some desk typing words on a screen. He couldn't think of anything more boring to do all day, except for maybe picking up trash, but at least doing that you got exercise.

Calvin Shoverton came to the Maxwells' house and watched them eat breakfast and get ready for school and did everything but follow them to the bathroom. (And he probably would have gone in there if they had left the door unlocked.) Tim overheard Kellen telling the writer that Jamie wasn't that bad of a big sister except when they traded licks, punching each other on the shoulder.

"I used to be able to hang in there for five or six rounds, but now it hurts too much," Kellen said. "She's gotten a lot stronger."

"She ever get full of herself?" Calvin said. "You know, pushy about how talented she is?"

Kellen laughed. "Jamie knows she's good, and she can handle herself on the track, but you'd never know by talking to her."

The writer guy nodded and wrote something down. Then he asked if he could ride with Jamie to school and talk. Jamie agreed, and Tim climbed into the backseat of her car. They spent most of the time talking about the old Mustang and how she'd rebuilt the engine from scratch. Tim thought the talk about the engine was the most interesting.

Calvin got out at school and took some pictures of Jamie near her car. He turned to Tim. "How about lunch?"

"It's a little early for that, isn't it?" Tim said.

Calvin chuckled. "No, I mean, why don't we have lunch together? My treat. We can grab a sub sandwich if you want. Mrs. Maxwell said that was your favorite. She gave her blessing."

"Okay." Tim shrugged.

Tim drifted through his morning classes, his stomach growling because he'd skipped breakfast. By lunch he was ravenous and would have eaten a horse-and-goat sub without any ketchup.

Calvin drove back to the school to pick up Tim.

"How'd you get your car?" Tim said.

"I had Dale pick me up after I interviewed a couple of teachers this morning."

"Teachers?" Tim said.

"Yeah, I wanted to hear what kind of student Jamie is. See if all the hype is worth it."

"What did you find out?"

"She seems like the real deal. Even went over to the church and talked with the youth pastor there. He said Jamie's gotten religious lately. Have you noticed that?"

"Yeah. She seems serious about it. But it's not like she wears burlap and eats locusts or anything. She's pretty normal."

"What about you?" Calvin said.

"What do you mean?"

"You believe the same way as the Maxwells? That God is good and we ought to follow him with our lives?"

Tim looked out the window. "This article's about Jamie, right? You don't want to know about me."

They stopped at the sub shop, and Tim ordered a foot-long with everything. They spread their sandwiches out at a picnic table near the strip mall.

Tim nearly choked on some lettuce and a hot pepper when Calvin said, "Must be quite a change living with the Maxwells instead of sleeping in Charlie Hale's hauler."

"How do you know about that?" was all Tim could think to say.

"This is my job. I ferret out information, write about it, and let people know what goes on inside the NASCAR world. I wrote a small piece about your dad, but there wasn't that much information about him and I didn't want to bother you so soon after his death. The team didn't even know where you'd been shipped off to."

"Did you find out?"

"Nice little trailer park in Florida. With Vera and Tyson, as I recall."

Tim's mouth dropped open. Then he closed it because he hadn't chewed.

"I felt like when the time was right, we could do a memorial article for him. Nothing fancy."

"I guess Dad wouldn't have wanted a big fuss, but something at the anniversary of the accident would be nice."

"Why'd the Maxwells take you in?"

Tim shrugged. "I think Dale felt bad about my dad. I don't think there's anything in it for them. My dad didn't have much money, so it wasn't about an inheritance."

Calvin smiled and munched on his sandwich. "Maxwell has a squeaky-clean image. Everybody knows where he stands on moral stuff. You ever see anything that's at odds with that?"

"You mean is he a hypocrite?"

Calvin nodded.

"He drives a big truck that guzzles gas." Tim leaned forward and whispered, "And I don't know if I should say this, but sometimes he eats leftover pizza for breakfast."

Calvin raised his eyebrows. "That's shocking."

"I know. I hope that doesn't get out 'cause it could ruin him."

Calvin shook his head and laughed. It seemed to Tim like he wasn't trying to write a story anymore. He was just enjoying his sandwich. That made Tim relax.

"So you're saying the stuff we see on the track and in front of the camera is basically what you see at home?"

Tim nodded. "They get into arguments and stuff like that. I mean, they're not perfect. Dale sometimes drives too fast, and Mrs. Maxwell tells him to slow down." He took a swig of soda. "So you just sit in front of a computer all day and type away on those little keys until you're done, huh?"

"A lot of my day is spent on the phone or traveling. I go to all the races. I listen to radio shows, watch TV. I get ideas from people who e-mail or call me. By the time I sit down at the computer, I've pretty much got the story written in my head."

Tim couldn't imagine all those words staying in a guy's head. Then he got an idea. "You say you're good at tracking people down. How good?"

"Depends on who the person is. Who are you looking for?"

Tim squinted at Calvin, wondering if he could trust him, and pulled a crumpled piece of paper out of his shirt pocket. "This is . . . what do you call it? You know, when you don't want somebody to write about something?"

"Off the record?"

"Yeah, that's it. Can this be off the record?"

Calvin held out a hand. "Let me see what you've got."

Chapter 8
Hickory

JAMIE TOOK THE BORROWED Late Model Stock car to Hickory for her next race. It had been a few weeks since she'd hit the track in Denver, and she was itching to get behind the wheel, even if it was a step down from where she wanted to be. Scotty's brother, Kyle, came along to act as crew chief. Tim would be her spotter.

Hickory, North Carolina, was a short jaunt up I-77 and then west on I-40. They hooked up the hauler to the Suburban in the dark and made it to the track just after sunrise. Tim helped, and Jamie's mom took care of the paperwork and kept Kellen settled, which was a full-time job.

Jamie recognized a few of the other racers, many of them twice her age, and said hello. When the drivers saw her, a few asked for an autograph.

One burly guy cinched up his pants and leaned against their hauler. "Look at this, Sonny," he said to a skinny guy with long sideburns. "You get to race against the great Jamie Maxwell. Future NASCAR queen."

After the inspection, it was time for a short practice session. The car was running rough, and when Jamie brought it back, Kyle discovered that the angle of the left front tire was wearing badly.

"Looks like we'll have to change the upper A-arm," Kyle said. "We don't and you won't make it through half the race."

Kyle crawled under the car, and with help from Tim, they felt ready for qualifying. Jamie turned in two good laps, though she said the car was loose in the turns. She qualified fourth for the race.

"I can't believe how many people know about you now," Kellen said to her as they waited for the start. "And you know they're going to be gunning for you."

"Why's that?"

"To say they beat a future cup winner," Kellen said. Then he imitated a guy spitting tobacco juice. "I 'member back when I raced that gal to the finish line. She was good but not as good as me."

Jamie chuckled. "I'm just glad I don't have to contend with Chad up here. . . ." Her voice trailed off as she looked down the line of competitors. A lanky guy walked past the line of cars, and she recognized the long arms before she even saw his face. “Thor?”

“Is that old Thunderfoot?” Kellen whispered.

Jamie nodded. “What are you doing here?” she said to Thor.

“You think you’re the only one who wants to race?” Thor said with a smirk. He looked at the car. “Heard about what happened in Denver. This your #62?”

“No, it’s a friend of mine’s.”

The radio clicked. “They’re calling for the drivers to get ready,” Kyle said.

“Guess I’ll see you out there on the track,” Jamie said.

Thor nodded. “You sure will.”

Kyle clicked the microphone when Jamie was buckled in. “You looking for some trouble from that guy in the #7 car?”

“He’s one of the top drivers from the school but likes to throw his weight around.”

“Watch him out there, you hear?” Kyle said.

Chapter 9
Spotter Surprise

TIM CLIMBED TO THE TOP of the grandstand and fiddled with the radio, trying to get it in a comfortable position on his head. He finally had to take off his hat, the one his dad had given him, and put it on a table in the back.

Not being a very talkative person, he felt a little nervous about guiding Jamie around the track. He'd been listening to spotters and crew chiefs ever since he was a little kid, though, and he knew the lingo as well as anyone. Plus, he wanted to see Jamie stay safe *and* win.

While he adjusted the volume control, someone walked up to him, blocking the sun and sending him into shadows.

"You're with the Maxwell team, aren't you?" a guy said. It was Kenny, one of the drivers at the experimental school. The one who had confronted Tim after Jamie made it into the final race.

Tim backed away, but he could only go so far from the spotter's station. The back of the building was a straight drop-off.

"Having some trouble with your volume control?" Kenny said. "Let me take a look at it."

Tim knew what was going to happen. Kenny was going to sabotage his radio—take the batteries or mix up the channels. Tim didn't want to give it up, but Kenny took it from him before he could react.

"You have the squelch turned all the way up," Kenny said, holding the radio out. "I cut it back for you. Should be good to go."

Tim stared at the radio like it was a dead fish, not believing that Kenny would actually help him. He took it and said, "Thanks."

"I'm spotting for Thunder, the #7 car. If you need anything, just yell, okay?"

Tim nodded and mustered a question. "Why are you being so nice? You hate me."

"I was really ticked off the last time I saw you. I was a jerk, all right? Heat of the battle and all that. You okay with that?"

Tim stared at Kenny, trying to analyze the situation. He felt about a foot tall next to the guy, not because Kenny was tall, but because he wore nice clothes, had sunglasses that probably cost more than some cars in the parking lot, and had an air about him that said, *I'm important*.

"Yeah, I've had those kinds of days myself," Tim finally said.

Kenny flashed a million-dollar smile—the kind you're not born with but pay for—patted Tim on the shoulder, and shook hands. "Good to hear, man. Your place is right over there. Good luck."

Tim took his spot and tested out the radio. Both Kyle and Jamie could hear him loud and clear.

"Don't be timid up there," Jamie said. "Speak up and we'll get each other through this."

"You'll never guess who I just talked with up here. Your old pal from the school. Kenny."

"What?" Jamie said.

It was at that point that he knew he needed to find quick access to the volume control because her voice nearly pierced his eardrums. Even the guys around him turned to look. Most of them had beer bellies and ancient hats with sweat stains that looked older than he was.

"All right, we're coming to the green flag," Tim said when the pace car peeled away. "You know what to do."

It was a single-file start, and as soon as the cars crossed the start/finish line, Tim could tell why the racing here was so popular. The people jumped to their feet, cheering as the engines screamed in a perfect blend of men (and girl) and machine. Tim took a quick look at the surrounding area—the trees and the rolling green around the track—and thought this would be a great place to live. He loved the sound of cars going fast.

Tim wasn't sure how much Jamie wanted him to talk, but things were so bunched up at the beginning of the race that there was nothing to tell her. When he saw she was clear on the outside or inside, he told her, but he didn't try to maneuver her around the track. She had been doing this a long time, and he didn't want to step on her toes.

"We've got a problem," Jamie said. "Engine's not firing right—like it lost a plug."

"Just one or more?" Kyle said.

"Feels like we've still got seven cylinders," Jamie said.

"We can go with seven on this track," Kyle said. "Keep the pedal down. You're looking good."

Tim kept his eye on Jamie's car, then remembered something Scotty had said about a spotter watching the whole track. On lap 40, just before the break in the race, a car in the middle of the pack got loose and crashed into the wall in turn three.

"Yellow flag," Tim said. "Got a few cars behind you in a problem."

"Ten-four," Jamie said.

The pace car came out. Then the red flag dropped. Tim alerted Jamie, and the entire field stopped in turn one.

"What's up?" Jamie said.

"The guy who hit the wall needs some medical attention," Tim said. "Hang tight."

Kenny came over to Tim and handed him a Coca-Cola. The top was off and Kenny was smiling. "Want a cold drink?"

Tim looked at it and something flashed in his brain—a memory he wanted to forget about Daytona and some "friends" who had turned out to be anything but. "No thanks," he said.

Chapter 10
Trouble

WHEN THE RACE RESUMED, Jamie could tell there was something seriously wrong with the car. She was fighting just to stay off the wall in the corners and losing spots with every lap.

"Keep at it," Kyle said. "Just two more laps and everybody comes in."

She strained with all her might to keep her speed up and stay in control, but the car was slowing. "I don't think it's the engine this time."

"Hang in there," Kyle said. "It could be vapor lock from being stopped out there."

"Doesn't sound like vapor lock if she's having trouble handling the car," Tim said.

"Yeah, it feels like a strut or something. I can't control the thing at speed."

"Hang on to it as best you can this

last lap," Kyle said. "We'll be ready for you when you get here."

Jamie limped into the pits. She helped Kellen with the fuel while Kyle jacked the car up and climbed under. She popped the hood and immediately saw a fried spark plug wire. They'd have to make it to the end down one cylinder.

From underneath came Kyle's muffled voice. "You were right. It's the rear axle. Spindle's out on the driver's side."

Jamie knew enough about that part of the car to realize she was done if they didn't get the spindle back in place. But if something was wrong inside, she'd have very little control. "Can you get it back in?"

"I can try, but if it comes loose again it's probably going to be worse. Like driving a bear chasing honeybees."

Tim ran into the pit area, breathing hard and white as a sheet. It looked like he'd run all the way from the grandstand. He glanced at Jamie, then got on his knees and looked under the car as Kyle explained the problem.

"Let me take a shot at it," Tim said. "If you slide it in and the sprockets find their place, there's a chance it'll be okay."

Jamie just shook her head at Tim. He went into mechanic mode as soon as he saw Kyle's tools. The track manager gave a signal for five minutes more on the pit stop. Then she saw Thor walking toward her. He was in first place and enjoying it.

"Having a rough time out there?" he said.

"Problem with the rear axle," Jamie said.

"Oh, that's not good. Too bad you won't be in the second half."

Tim scooted out from under the car. "She'll be there." He scooted back under again.

Thor smiled and cocked his head. "Well, guess I'd better mosey back to my ride and see if I can't get another win."

Jamie rolled her eyes. "Just don't get too comfortable up there."

Kyle stood and wiped the grease from his hands. "Where'd you get this Tim kid? He's an animal under there—like he was born with an air wrench in his hand."

Jamie smiled. "I think he picked a lot of it up just watching. You think we'll be ready for the restart?"

Before Kyle could answer, Tim slid out from under the car. "Good to go. You'll have to take the whole back end apart to fix it right, but this may get you to the end of the race."

Tim loped off to the infield, and Jamie climbed into the car.

"Glad Tim's the one running to the spotter stand," Kyle said. "I wouldn't have enough breath left for the rest of the race."

Chapter 11
Perseverance

TIM MADE IT BACK to his grandstand spot two laps after the restart. He didn't catch his breath for another 10 laps. He'd heard Jamie tell Kyle that the handling was a lot better and she was up to full speed. Tim was impressed that Jamie had checked the plug. Lots of drivers didn't know much about what was under the hood. They just wanted to shift gears and mash their feet to the floor. Tim knew the best ones made themselves part of the car, and when they felt something wrong, they knew what was going on.

Jamie made her way through the crowd and to the front, just behind the #7 car.

Tim looked at Kenny as he spoke to Thor.

"She's right on your tail, buddy,"

Kenny said. "Stay on the inside and make her go high. It's a longer track that way."

Jamie stayed with Thor until lap 65, when she went wildly outside and almost into the wall in turn two. "Got a problem. Feels like the same thing."

"Spindle must have popped out again," Tim said.

"We've got 35 laps to go," Kyle said. "You want to bring it in or stay out there?"

"If I bring it in, I'm giving up. I'll stay here."

Tim smiled and felt a shiver run down his spine. Jamie sure had spunk.

Seven laps later, Jamie was at the back of the pack with Thor running up on her bumper. Tim knew she hated to be lapped, but she couldn't get up to speed like she normally would because in the turns she simply lost control of the rear end. Her left rear tire was on its own.

"Better let him pass," Tim said. "Stay low and let him go on the outside."

Jamie growled. "I hate this."

"I hoped the spindle would hold until the end," Tim said. "Sorry about that."

"No, it's not your fault. I just hate losing to this guy."

Tim glanced at Kenny, who was grinning, and clicked the microphone. "I know what you mean."

Jamie finished in ninth place. When Tim told one of the other spotters that she had done it down a cylinder and an axle, he couldn't believe it. Tim figured word would spread and this would add to the respect the other drivers and teams had for her. And who could blame them?

It was the kind of race the youth pastor would talk about in church—pleasing God by hanging in there and sticking with something to the end. He'd probably even have a verse about persevering through hard times. It almost made Tim want to believe it was true.

He went back to the table to retrieve his hat, but it wasn't there. He looked behind the table and on the floor, thinking the hat might have blown down there, but he couldn't find it. He was sick inside, and though it pained him, he turned and asked a few people if they had seen it. He described it in detail. "It's just an old hat. I don't know why anybody would want to steal it."

Nobody had seen it.

Tim moved to the railing and looked down on the people filing out. The hat was gone. It was just gone.

Chapter 12
Mrs. Dagsnit

JAMIE COULDN'T BELIEVE all the press coverage her dad got for his miraculous move into the Chase. Only once before had anyone leapfrogged over so many drivers in the last few races to make it. Never in the history of the Chase had anyone squeezed into the 12th spot and then claimed the cup.

The Calvin Shoverton article had run two weeks after New Hampshire, where her dad had placed sixth. He'd been leading till the final 50 laps, and then an accident forced him to the pits. He was hit square in the back, though, and after taking the crush panels out, he fought his way back to the sixth spot. Because he'd led so many laps, his point totals pushed him into the ninth position.

The article had centered on her dad, of course, but there was a lot in there about Jamie as well as Tim. He came off as the outcast orphan taken in by the loving family, and while that was partly true, Jamie thought the picture Shoverton painted made her family look too saintly. He wrote:

Very little is known about the life Tim Carhardt led between his father's death and his move to Velocity, NC. There were a few months spent living with a distant cousin, and to hear Tim talk about it, it was simply a blip on the radar screen of his life.

But if you look closely, the deep wounds of Talladega and a mother who all but disappeared into thin air have shaped this young man. And to hear Dale Maxwell talk about him is like hearing a doting father talk about a gifted son. Almost like you're hearing Tim's real father speak.

"Tim's a great kid who had something tough happen," Dale said, his eyes filling as he spoke. "I felt so bad after the accident and wanted to give him a chance at something new and to let him know that his life doesn't have to be defined by one event. I couldn't be more proud of the way he's handled everything if he were my own son."

/////

Before English class one day, Vanessa Moran found Jamie and shoved the article in front of her. "I don't get this."

"Get what?" Jamie said, handing the article back to her.

"Lots of stuff. Like, how do they keep score in NASCAR? None of it makes sense to me."

"You've been watching the races?" Jamie said, smiling.

"Yeah, my dad has a few clients who are drivers or crew chiefs or whatever you call them. And we got tickets to the Charlotte race in October."

"So you're into it?" Jamie said. "I can't believe it."

"I'm into the cute drivers and the hunky-looking crew members and the strategy and teamwork and . . ." Vanessa sighed. "I just can't understand how to make sense of the scoring. How did your dad jump up so much without winning the race?"

Jamie nodded. "It's kind of complicated—and they seem to change the points system just about every year—but basically you get a certain amount of points if you win a race, and then second place gets a few less points, and on down the line. Plus, you have to factor in the lap leaders. They get extra points for laps led and who leads the most laps."

"You need to go to a race with a calculator," Vanessa said.

"Almost, but they keep track of all that for you. That's one of the things that makes each lap so exciting. It's not just cars circling the track where it only gets interesting at the end. It's team members trying to help each other out, and it's solo drivers like my dad trying to wiggle into the top 12. All that comes together at every race."

Vanessa looked at the story. "Yeah, I'm starting to see that. There's just one thing that gets me."

"What?"

Other students filed into the classroom, and the hallway was almost empty. Their English teacher, Mrs. Dagsnit (a few kids called her Mrs. Dogbit), didn't like kids being late.

"It's the whole spiritual thing," Vanessa said. "I've been going to the youth group since we moved here, and you've always seemed like a levelheaded person. You didn't take the whole Christian thing over the edge like some people do."

"I'm not sure I know what you mean," Jamie said.

"You know Cassie and Pastor Gordon and a few others act like you have to give your whole life to God and go off to some foreign country if you really want to be a Christian. But you're different. You've acted like it's okay to believe in God but not to let it ruin your life. Then I read in this article that you've had some big spiritual renewal."

The bell rang, and Mrs. Dagsnit gave them the evil eye.

"Why don't we talk at lunch?" Jamie said.

Chapter 13
Calvin's News

TIM WALKED OUTSIDE the school to eat his lunch. Mrs. Maxwell had him make his own lunch, just like Jamie and Kellen. It was no problem for him because he'd done that in Florida without much help from the Slades. At least here at the Maxwells' house they had a drawer full of chips and snacks, plus plenty of bread and meat for sandwiches. And Mrs. Maxwell sure did like to cut up celery and carrots.

Tim sat under a tree that looked like it couldn't figure out what color it wanted to be. This time of year in North Carolina the leaves looked like a new box of Crayolas. Every color under the sun and then some.

A few football players and cheerleaders sat at a picnic table several yards away. There was a lot of talk about the Velocity High football team, but Tim didn't know much about it. He hadn't been to any games and didn't want to go. He figured he had very little chance of becoming friends with that crowd anyway.

He pulled out his cell phone as he took a bite of a ham sandwich. He'd been given the phone by the Maxwells in order to get in touch with them if he missed the bus and needed a ride or had some other emergency. It wasn't fancy, just a prepaid phone that charged 20 cents a minute, but he didn't have anybody to text and he wasn't going to phone Tyson in Florida.

The screen said "1 message waiting." He retrieved it and listened. It was the writer, Calvin Shoverton. "Hey, Tim, sorry it's taken me so long to get back to you. I have good and bad news. Call me." He gave his number and Tim dialed him back.

"Well, first I want you to know this is a hard one," Calvin said. "It took me several days to get the public records people down there to tell me what I needed to know. I finally got in touch with a reporter. . . ."

Tim watched the time tick by. He noticed his heart was beating faster and he was sweating a little.

Finally, Calvin said the magic word *but*. ". . . but I did track down the court case of your mom." He sounded like he was reading from some official document. "Alexandra Lee Burton Carhardt was committed to the Kathryn A. Ross Women's Correctional Facility three years ago. She was released in January of this year. Her parole officer is almost as hard to find as she is. She said your mom came to see her for two months after she got out and hasn't been seen since. So there's an arrest warrant out for her in Florida."

"Why was she put in prison?" Tim said.

Calvin paused. "It was a drug offense. I tracked down the actual court proceedings. There was a blurb in a paper down there that said she was convicted of drug trafficking."

"What does that mean?"

"Looks like she was working for a limousine service and tried to put drugs in somebody's luggage without them knowing it. I don't know much more about the specifics, but she pleaded guilty."

"So you have no idea where she is now?" Tim said.

"Zilch, zero, nada. Like a puff of smoke in the wind. Just disappeared."

"Any guesses?"

"I talked with a police officer friend, and he said that anybody who would skip parole probably wouldn't stick around the state. It's hard telling where she went. She could have caught a bus to New York or headed west. If she wants to stay invisible, she can. At least for a while."

A cloud passed over the school, and Tim felt a chill go through him. "You put a lot of work into this, and I'm grateful."

"Didn't do much at all. Did you see the article?"

"Yeah, you're a good writer."

"What did you really think?" Calvin said.

"Well, it kinda made me look like some poor orphan kid people ought to feel sorry for, you know? Like a wayward youth who gets picked up by some Bible-thumpers who are doing their good deed for the decade."

Calvin laughed. "That's not a bad analysis."

"I'm not saying what you wrote wasn't true," Tim said. "It just wasn't the whole story."

"I got you. I guess an article is like a snapshot—we can only capture a little of the story at a time. Thanks for the feedback. How about the Maxwells? What did they think?"

"I don't think Jamie liked the quotes from Kellen. She chased him around the house threatening to rearrange his teeth, but I don't think she will. And Mrs. Maxwell cut the article out and put it in the scrapbook she keeps. I took a look at their hall closet, and the thing is about full floor to ceiling with those things."

Calvin chuckled again, and then a voice came on Tim's phone that said he had only five minutes of air time left.

"I gotta go, Mr. Shoverton. Thanks for the information about my mom."

"You bet. Call me anytime, and if I find out anything else, I'll let you know."

Chapter 14
Lunch with Vanessa

JAMIE MADE IT THROUGH the lunch line and picked up some fruit and a container of yogurt. Mixed berry was her favorite, but the closest she could come was strawberry banana. She grabbed a plastic spoon and found Vanessa in the commons near the big palm tree.

They made small talk about their day and Jamie tried to act natural, but she couldn't help feeling nervous. Since the talk with her dad about spiritual things, she'd been praying for her friends who weren't Christians, and Vanessa was at the top of the list. Jamie was also studying the Bible—not just reading it but studying it—with a couple of books Cassie suggested.

Vanessa's question about Jamie's spiritual life was an answer to prayer—but also an opportunity to say something stupid, and she didn't want to do that. She almost felt like a dog that had chased a car and caught it and now didn't know what to do with it.

She took a deep breath and tried to relax. *Just another conversation with a friend,* she thought.

"So what did you think about what I said?" Vanessa asked.

"You nailed me," Jamie said. "If you'd have asked me last spring what God meant to me, I'd have said that he was great and awesome and blah, blah, blah. But I wouldn't have known what I was talking about. Now I can say it from the heart."

"What happened to you?"

Jamie sighed. "I've always thought of God as just 'the good Lord,' you know? Up there somewhere, not really caring about what we do down here—unless we do something wrong or have fun, and then he comes down hard on us. He makes us feel guilty or gives us cancer or takes away something we love."

"Yeah," Vanessa said. "I know exactly what you mean. But what changed?"

"I guess I got a good look at myself. My god was racing. I love being in that cockpit, and I really want to be the best and go the fastest. I thought if I gave my life to God, he'd take my dreams away and make me do something I hated."

Vanessa stared at her natural soda. "And now you think differently?"

Jamie nodded. “My dad helped me see it. God wants what is absolutely best for me. If I follow his plan, I’ll wind up a lot more happy and fulfilled than I will if I follow my own. Now, I’m kind of new at this, so I’m not saying I think that way all the time, but I really want what he wants.”

“You think that involves racing?” Vanessa said.

“I hope so. But I guess part of submitting to God is trusting him and waiting. I think he’s given me a gift—an ability he wants to use. I don’t know how, but I’m along for the ride.”

“Wow,” Vanessa said, but it didn’t sound very convincing.

“Have you ever done that?” Jamie said. “Asked God to come into your life and forgive you?”

Vanessa picked up her half-full soda can and tossed it into the nearby trash can. “I have to go. I’ll see you around.”

“Vanessa?” Jamie called, but the girl was gone.

Chapter 15
A Bad Scene

TIM AND KELLEN WATCHED the Dover race together in the garage and cheered as Dale finished ninth. Another top 10 was good, and the fact that several cup contenders finished 20th or lower helped Dale move up to the eighth position, but the big drawback was that Butch Devalon had finished first and was now second in the Chase.

"We started the year strong, and we're going to finish the year strong," Devalon said as he spread some liquid on the crowd around him. He cursed, then said, "We've got the best team and the fastest car, so all I have to do is go out and make it happen."

"I'd do anything to make sure that guy doesn't win," Tim said. "I wish he'd get in a big wreck and get stuck in his car for the rest of the season. Then they can pull him out."

"Better not let Dad hear you talk like that," Kellen said. "He says Butch has every right to be where he is and to crow all he wants."

"Well, I'd like to go crow hunting," Tim said, and Kellen laughed.

Sunday evening Tim did some of his homework in his room and didn't go to the airport to pick up Dale. He was supposed to write a paper for English on what he'd do with a million dollars. He began the essay with:

Probably everybody in class will write that they would give a million dollars to charity so they can feel good about themselves. While they can do what they want, I wouldn't give to save whales or fight global warming or anything like that. I would use the money to open up a garage so I could fix people's cars that are broken down. And it would be a good investment because I'd probably have to hire somebody to answer the phone and at least two other people to work with me because a lot of cars need repairs. And when single moms come in, I'd give them a discount and wouldn't charge them as much.

Tim sat back and looked at his words. He wished he were Calvin Shoverton's kid and could ask his dad advice on what to say. He started again.

If I had a million dollars, I would give it away to Camp Left Turn. They give sick kids the chance to spend a few days riding horses and swimming and just acting like normal kids. I went there in July, and when you see the faces of those kids, it just makes your heart happy. I would probably save a little bit for myself to maybe buy a car or start a business, but most of it I would give to that camp.

Tim figured the teacher would like this better, so he crumpled up the first one and tossed it. His cell phone rang, and he thought it was probably Mrs. Maxwell asking if he wanted something for dessert on their way home from the airport. Strange, because she usually called the house phone for stuff like that. Plus, the phone number showed up as "unknown number."

"Hello?"

There was a fumbling with the phone, like someone was passing it to a different person.

"Hello?" Tim said again.

A pause. "Tim?" a female voice said.

"Yeah, this is Tim."

"Timmy, I need to see you."

A shiver went down his back. His dad said his mom used to call him Timmy, though he couldn't remember much about that. "Who is this?"

"Son, I think you know, don't you?" she said.

Tim sat up. "Mom?"

"I want you to write down this address, and I want you to meet me there in 20 minutes."

"I don't have a car."

"It's not that far away," the woman said. "Do you have a bike?"

"I can borrow one," Tim said.

She gave him the address, and he wrote it down. He thought the street sounded familiar, but he couldn't place it.

"I'll see you in 20 minutes," she said. "Don't be late."

"Wait. I need to know—"

The line went dead, and Tim hung up and hurried to the computer. He plugged in the address and printed out a map, then headed outside to Kellen's bike.

The air was brisk and chilly, but Tim didn't care. He pedaled as fast as he could and raised a sweat as he rode past a main road. He cut across a dirt road, ducking low-hanging tree limbs, and steered his way through a field and onto pavement. He stopped under a streetlight to make sure he was on the right track, checking the location and starting again.

Over the years, Tim had thought he had seen his mom several times in crowds, at races, and even in restaurants. In fact, on the day his dad had died, he thought he saw her in the stands and had followed and found it was someone else. Each time he was disappointed. Now, at last, he hoped to see her and find out why she had left him and his dad.

He found the street and raced down it, clicking his stopwatch to see that it had taken exactly 18 minutes to get here. He slid to a stop in front of a large iron gate with the address over it, the same one the woman—was it his mom?—had given on the phone. He looked around and saw no one on the road, so he leaned the bike against the gate. He paced a few steps, then heard movement on gravel nearby.

"Hello?" he called. "Anybody in there?"

No answer.

Tim studied the gate. It didn't look electrified, and there was no razor wire at the top. He didn't hear any dogs inside, so he took a chance and scaled the gate, dropping to the other side. He tweaked his ankle coming down and hopped toward the building at the end of the driveway. In the dim light of the streetlamp he could see the black *13* on the front of the building. At that moment, something other than seeing his mother entered his mind—something scary that reminded him of a car pulling up behind him in Florida and people getting out and jumping him. His instincts told him he was in trouble.

He turned to run but caught sight of a flickering flame at the back of the building. Stopping, he squinted to see if the flicker was inside or outside the building. He moved to the side, walking gingerly on his ankle, and cupped his hands around his eyes so he could see inside the garage. The flames were inside!

Tim took out his cell phone and dialed 911, but just as he did, he heard a siren wailing and saw red lights flash in the distance. He clicked off his phone and hobbled back toward the gate, but before he reached it, an explosion rocked the area, smashing glass and sending it skittering on the concrete near him.

Tim hit the ground and stayed there until the shower of debris stopped. As the fire truck neared, he climbed over the fence, landed again on his hurt ankle, and headed back the way he had come. Behind him, he heard shouts of the firemen trying to get inside the gate. He didn't stop pedaling until he pulled into the Maxwells' garage and found Dale there.

"Where've you been so late?" Dale said.

"Just went for a ride," Tim said. "Good job at the race."

"Thanks."

"If it's okay with you, I got an early day tomorrow. I'm going to bed."

"Okay, Tim. See you in the morning."

Chapter 16

Officer Dunham

WHEN JAMIE DROVE Tim to school the next day, he was unusually quiet. Not that he was very talkative most of the time, but he just stared out the window. She turned up the radio as a news report about a fire the night before was coming on.

". . . top story concerns a mysterious fire at the Butch Devalon Racing complex," the reporter said. "An explosion there last night blew out some windows, but authorities say they were able to save the structure. The fire is suspicious in origin. It comes only a few hours after Devalon won a race in Dover, Delaware."

Jamie reached for the volume knob and turned it down. "Wow, I hadn't heard anything about—"

"No, listen," Tim said, leaning over and turning up the radio.

". . . and authorities say they have possible leads about the person or persons who may be involved. We'll have more about that in our eight o'clock hour and an interview with Butch Devalon then as well."

Jamie turned the radio off. "That's weird. Who would want to burn down Devalon's garage?"

Tim shrugged.

Jamie went from school to the gym. She only worked part-time at the auto parts store and her shift didn't begin until six, so she wanted to get in a good work-out beforehand.

When she got home, she was surprised to see a police car in the driveway. Her dad was on the front porch with the officer, and Kellen was talking to them.

"What's up?" Jamie said as she walked over.

"Do you know where Tim is?" her dad said, his face grim.

"No. He takes the bus home."

The officer tipped his hat and crossed his arms in front of him. "Jamie, I've admired your driving. Think I'll be admiring it even more in the years to come."

"Thanks," she said. "What's this all about?"

The officer took a deep breath. "Did Tim seem himself this morning when you drove to school?"

Jamie pursed her lips. "He was pretty quiet. Of course, he doesn't say much to begin with. . . ." She thought a moment. "He did get squirrelly about the news report we heard on the radio."

"What report was that?" her dad said.

"The Devalon garage fire. He seemed really interested in it."

The reaction of all three was immediate. Her dad shook his head, the officer nodded, and Kellen closed his eyes and tipped his head back, like his favorite team had just lost the Super Bowl by a last-second field goal.

"What?" Jamie said.

"They think Tim might have been involved in the fire," her dad said.

"That's crazy!" Jamie said. "Tim wouldn't do anything like that."

"That's not what your brother says," the officer said.

"Tell her," her dad said to Kellen.

Kellen looked like he had sold his favorite horse to a dog food factory. "Tim was talking during the race about Devalon, saying some wild stuff. I don't think he's capable of hurting a flea—"

"What did he say?" Jamie said.

"Something about making sure Devalon didn't win and getting stuck in his car or something dumb like that. He was just kidding around—he didn't mean anything by it."

"Yeah, well, here he comes," Jamie's dad said.

Tim walked past the squad car, taking a good look at the exhaust and (Jamie thought) imagining what the engine looked like. He walked tentatively, like an animal going to slaughter.

"Tim, this is Officer Dunham," her dad said. "You have any idea why he's here?"

"Should I?" Tim said.

"Were you at the Devalon racing complex last night?" the officer said.

Tim hesitated. "I might have driven Kellen's bike over that way." He glanced at Kellen. "I didn't think you'd mind."

"No problem," Kellen said.

"Did you go on their property?"

Tim looked away and put his hands in his pockets.

"Maybe we should get legal counsel on this," Jamie's dad said.

"No, it's okay," Tim said. "I'll tell you what happened. I went over there and climbed the fence. That's when I saw the fire inside, and as I was about to call 911, the fire trucks got there and I took off. I was scared somebody would pin the thing on me."

Officer Dunham stared at him. "And you expect us to believe you didn't start the fire."

"It was burning when I got there, sir."

"Why did you go there?" the officer said.

Tim put his toe in the dust, and he looked to Jamie like a little kid who had forgotten his fishing pole at the Boy Scout campout. He looked at Jamie's dad and searched for words. "It's kind of personal."

"Trying to burn down a garage complex is kind of personal—don't you think?" the officer said.

"I didn't burn anything," Tim said.

Jamie's dad searched Tim's face. "Son, I think we're going to need more than that. There must have been some reason you went over there that late. Why can't you tell us?"

"I got a phone call," Tim said haltingly. "I don't know who it was. They just gave me the address, and I rode over there."

"Must've been someone pretty important," Officer Dunham said.

"Yeah," Tim said.

"A girlfriend of yours?" the officer said.

Jamie studied her dad, who studied Tim. It was almost like he could see right through him.

"Officer, let me talk with Tim," her dad said. "You want us to come down to the station with you?"

The officer took off his hat, showing a huge bald spot, and scratched the top of his head. He walked over to the squad car, opened it, and pulled something off the front seat. "You'll probably want to explain this when you get there," he said, holding up a hat inside a plastic bag.

"That's mine," Tim said. "My dad gave it to me. Where'd you find it?"

Officer Dunham put the bag back into the car. "Inside the building. Near where the explosion happened."

Tim's mouth dropped open, and he looked like he was computing things in his head. Jamie felt bad for him. All the evidence pointed to his guilt, but she couldn't imagine him setting fire to Butch Devalon's palace of a garage.

"Oh," the officer said as he got inside his car, "you'll want to explain the surveillance video we have of you there too." He drove away.

Kellen came up beside Tim and put an arm on his shoulder. "They're not sending him to prison, are they, Dad?"

"Nobody's going to prison. There's a good explanation for this. I just don't know what it is."

Chapter 17
Dale and Tim

TIM SAT ON HIS BED and stared at the ceiling. Dale leaned against the wall, his arms crossed.

"So this is basically you being in the wrong place at the wrong time," Dale said.

"Big-time," Tim said.

Dale scratched the back of his neck. "I want to believe you. And I think you told the truth to that officer, and that must have been hard. But I also think you're holding back something important. Is there anything you want to tell me about what happened?"

"Like what?"

"Like, I don't know, that you just got so mad at the whole Devalon thing and you went into a rage and . . ."

"How would I have gotten into that

locked building?" Tim said. "Wouldn't they have found a broken window or something?"

"There was a broken window," Dale said. "On the other side of the garage. That set off an alarm, and a company called the building manager, who lives across the street. He saw the fire and called the fire department."

It's the hat, Tim thought. *If I can figure out who got my hat . . .*

"What are you thinking, Tim? I can't help you if you don't let me."

Tim had been in this situation a few times before when he'd had problems with the authorities. Once a police officer came to Tyson's place after Tim had smashed the mailbox of some people who were giving him trouble. Tim finally admitted he did it and agreed to buy and install a new mailbox after school the next day. He had done it, though he hadn't liked standing in front of the other trailer, listening to the people inside say mean things about him. And then there was his run-in with Jeff and the slashing of tires in the church parking lot that turned out to be the pastor's car.

Now Tim had to make a choice. Either let Dale inside or try to handle the whole thing himself. Tim could tell there was a part of Dale that didn't believe him, but it seemed like there was a part of him that did.

"You've got enough on your mind with the Chase," Tim said. "I don't want to drag you into this."

"You're not dragging me into anything. I'm already in. And I want to be in. There's nothing more important than helping you get on the right track. Talk to me."

Tim wished Mrs. Maxwell were here. He could make a face and she would just melt. She always felt so sorry for him, but Dale was a lot stronger and wouldn't be moved by a whimper or hangdog look. The guy had a lot of compassion, but he had backbone too.

"Who called you on your cell?" Dale said.

"I don't know who it was, but I thought it was . . . somebody else."

"Male? Female?"

"Female. Kind of older sounding. Or somebody trying to sound older."

"What did she say?"

"That I was supposed to come over to that address and meet her."

Dale thought a minute and squatted next to the wall. "This isn't about your mother, is it?"

Tim was surprised he'd put it together so fast. He nodded.

Dale's face scrunched up so much that Tim thought he wouldn't have been more surprised if Tim had said it was the Queen of England asking him for a date. At a truck and tractor pull.

Tim sighed and spilled the story about Calvin Shoverton and what he had learned about his mom. "I've been thinking a lot about her lately, so when that lady called on the phone, I kind of bit like a hungry fish."

Dale stood and leaned against the wall. His muscles tensed and he shook his head. "I can't believe anybody would do that to you."

"What do you mean?" Tim said.

"Set you up like that. Draw you over there that way."

"You believe me?"

"When did you lose your hat?"

"The race at Hickory. I set it down on a table so I could adjust my headset, and after the race it was gone."

"Who was on that grandstand?"

Tim told him some of the people. "But those are only the ones I can remember. A lot of people were up there."

Dale thought a moment.

Tim sat up. "No fair not telling me what's going on in your head."

Dale smiled, and Tim thought it was funny how

much a smile could say. This one said, *Okay, you rascal, you got me on that one.*

"All right," Dale said. "I want you to tell me exactly what happened from the minute you got the call. And give me your cell phone."

Chapter 18
Kansas Speedway

JAMIE FLEW with her dad to Kansas and took a couple of days off from school. She could tell the situation with Tim was weighing on him and she didn't want to pry, but when she asked a question, he told her a lot about what was going on with the police and their investigation.

"The surveillance video inside the building cuts out," her dad said. "The police said it had been tampered with. But the video of Tim as he comes up to the building . . ." He choked up.

"What?"

He turned his head, then looked at her with misty eyes. "The video was blurry, but you could see the hope on that kid's face. He actually thought he was going to see his mom. He goes to the side of the building for a few seconds and runs by—then there's the explosion. He never sets foot in the building. The whole thing was a setup. It had to be."

"But the police don't believe that?"

"They're not saying much about it. It's clear they're looking for the person who set the fire."

"Who called Tim?"

"They couldn't trace the cell call, and for the life of me I can't think why anyone would want to hurt a kid that way. Tim mentioned some guy in Florida he had trouble with, but that doesn't seem very likely."

"Maybe it's somebody who hates both you and Devalon," Jamie said. "I can think of a lot of people who don't like Butch, but the list is a little shorter when it comes to you. They could say you put Tim up to it and take both you and Devalon out with one fire."

"They didn't do a very good job of it. I'm going to have a talk with Devalon when we get to the race. He wouldn't return my phone call."

"What are you going to say?"

"The truth. That Tim wasn't involved. The police have spoken to him, but I want him to hear it from me. Plus, Talladega's coming up next week and I want Tim there. It's not fair to keep him away because he made a mistake back at Indy."

"Does Tim even want to go to Talladega?"

"Yeah, he said he'd like to honor his dad. Said it would feel good to be back."

"That takes some guts. If anything ever happened to you, I don't know if . . ."

"Nothing's gonna happen."

Jamie turned, deep in thought, and grabbed a magazine from the pouch in front of her. She flipped through the pages, unable to concentrate on any articles, and came upon an advertisement for a natural supplement that was "guaranteed" to help you focus and stay on task. Just one pill would help a person get more done in a day than most people do in a week.

She put the magazine down. "Maybe that's what this whole thing is about. Somebody wants to distract you from the Chase."

"And they're using Tim? And Devalon? I can't see it. Everybody's watching the teams out there like a hawk. This seems like somebody just wants to be mean."

"What about Devalon himself?" Jamie said.

Her dad shook his head. "Why would he want to destroy his own garage? Doesn't make sense."

When they arrived at the Kansas Speedway, Jamie and her dad went straight to the haulers and located the Devalon crew. They pointed out Devalon's RV in the infield.

"Maybe I should do this alone," her dad said.

"I think I'll tag along just for fun," Jamie said. "I love

seeing the veins in your neck stick out. And your face get red. And your eyes bugging out so far—"

"That's enough," he said.

Her dad knocked on the RV door, and Mrs. Devalon walked to the front. When she saw the two of them through the window, her mouth dropped open, and she turned and hurried back inside the RV.

"I don't think that was exactly a warm welcome," Jamie said.

She laughed, but she got quiet when a guy who looked twice the size of her dad came to the door. Arms like tree trunks. A barrel chest. A neck that looked more like a slice out of a telephone pole.

"Can I help you?" the man said in an unusually high-pitched voice.

Her dad reached out a hand, but the guy just looked at it like it was a dead opossum and kept his hands tucked into his armpits.

"I'm Dale Maxwell. Just wanted to have a word with Butch."

The guy stared through his Bollé sunglasses.

"It's a personal matter," her dad said. "I'd appreciate it if you'd tell him I'd like to speak with him."

"I can do that, but I'd like you to step away from the door, please."

Jamie looked at her dad and stepped back. When the guy left, she said, "I didn't know Butch needed a bodyguard. And his voice didn't match his body at all."

"Maybe his first name's Mickey." Her dad paced, kicking at clods of dirt and shoving his hands in his pockets.

When "Mickey" returned (Jamie smiled at the thought of calling him that), he was alone. "Mr. Devalon is not available right now. I'm sorry."

"Could you have him stop by my hauler later? Or just have him call me on my cell?" Her dad handed the man a card, and this time he took it but quickly stuffed it in his pocket—sort of like the dead opossum you put in your pocket without looking at it.

"I'll tell him, Mr. Maxwell, but you need to know that because of the cloud of suspicion around the boy staying with you and for legal reasons, Mr. Devalon won't be communicating with you."

Her dad looked like he wanted to say something else, like he wanted to chew the guy out, but he held back. He simply tipped his hat to Mickey and walked away.

A few hours later, when Devalon was returning from a practice run, Jamie saw her dad step out from one of the garage stalls right in front of him. Devalon tried to avoid him, but her dad blocked him. Devalon pointed a finger in her dad's face, and now it was his turn for his neck veins to stand out and his face to get red. Jamie hurried over in time to hear part of the conversation.

". . . and I don't care what it takes. I'm going to make sure he gets what's coming to him!" Devalon yelled.

"Butch, be reasonable," her dad said. "Tim had nothing to do with what happened. He was lured there by someone who called him—"

"That's *his* story, and I'm surprised a guy like you would buy it."

"Calm down."

"Don't tell me what to do, and get out of my way."

A crowd had begun to gather around the two, and a camera crew shooting something at another garage stall came over and caught the argument. Jamie could see exactly what would happen on the broadcast and what people would be talking about on the radio tonight. They'd throw fuel on the fire of the Butch and Dale "feud."

"Look," her dad said in a low tone. "I want you to know I'm sorry about the fire. I'm glad none of your cars were damaged. I know you'll see in the end that Tim had nothing to do with it. And with the anniversary of his dad's death, I hope you'll agree that he should be at Talladega next week."

Devalon stared daggers at her dad. "He'll be in the pits over my dead body." He stalked away and the camera followed. He angrily picked up his phone and clicked the intercom. Before he got out of camera range, Mickey showed up, craning his neck to see behind Devalon and looking like a human apology.

Jamie's dad walked past her and grunted, "That went well."

Chapter 19
Scrawled Writing

TIM STAYED IN HIS ROOM or went to the Maxwell garage most of the weekend. Mrs. Maxwell had let him take a day off from school the week of the fire, and he spent it looking at maps of places where he could run away. Maybe his mom had a good idea after all. She had run from Florida, and it hadn't caught up with her. Maybe he would do the same.

Still, the advantages the Maxwells offered him—not just the nice room, three squares a day, and a family atmosphere he'd never had but also the chance to work with an actual race team and the prospects for his future—were all hard to leave. It just seemed that no matter where he lived, no matter how hard he tried, the world was against him. And the people who were his friends paid for it.

On Saturday Tim heard the mailman pass and drive off. Mrs. Maxwell and Kellen had gone to some car wash the Sunday school was having at the church. The money was supposed to go to save orphans on Mars or something like that, and Tim said he'd pass when they invited him to tag along.

There was a box from the local bank—some checks Mrs. Maxwell had ordered—the latest issue of *NASCAR Scene* magazine, the water bill, and a few fan letters. At the bottom of the stack in a plain white envelope was a letter addressed to *Tim Carhardt,* written in pencil.

Finally somebody knows how to spell my last name, Tim thought.

He opened it on his way to the house and unfolded the piece of notebook paper. The letter was written in pencil too, on the front and the back, and the handwriting was scrawled, like somebody who had bad arthritis had written it. Either that or a really intelligent monkey at the zoo.

Timmy,

I suppose you knew this letter would come at some point. And if you're wondering, I saw a write-up about you and the Maxwells in one of those NASCAR fan magazines. That's how I got the idea to write. I can tell you how I got the address at a later time.

I haven't been a very good mother. I haven't been a mother at all. I wish I could make up for all those years behind us, but I don't think I can. I just wanted you to know that I'm sorry for walking out on you when you were little. Sure wish I could take that decision back and have a do-over. I wish I could make my whole life a do-over.

I read about what happened last year at Talladega. I went looking for you in Florida, but you weren't where I thought. Then I saw the article about the Maxwell family. They look like really nice people. To take you in, they'd have to be, right? Yuk, yuk.

I hope one day you'll be able to find it in your heart to forgive me, but I know that's too much to ask for in the first letter. I've made a lot of mistakes, but the one thing I know is you're not one of them. Even though I was really far away, there wasn't a day that I didn't think about you and wonder what you were doing or if you ever thought of me.

I have this dream every now and then that

you're playing by a swing set and then you get on and ask me to push you, but for some reason I can't. My feet and my arms are stuck where I am, and I want to move toward you, but something is holding me back. Well, I don't want to live in that dream anymore, and I hope that one day I can reach out to you and give you a push or a hug.

I hope you're doing okay. I'll be in touch with you again. If you don't want to see me, I'll understand.

Love,

Mom

Tim lingered on the top step and read the letter again. Then he sat down on the porch swing and re-read it. No matter how scrawled the writing was, it was still from his mother. No matter how much she had done to hurt him, this was still the one he had looked for in crowds and at races all these years.

He flipped the envelope over and saw the post-mark on the front that said, *Aiken, SC.*

Not a bad name for the way she feels, he thought. *Or me. Why wouldn't she have left a phone number? Unless she was afraid somebody would find this and track her down. . . .*

A car passed and he glanced at it. The phone call on his cell, the woman who said she was his mom—that couldn't have been his real mother, could it? She wasn't trying to make it up to him by destroying the Devalon garage, was she?

He shook the thought away and took the rest of the mail inside. He went to Mrs. Maxwell's desk and found her calendar open and a star beside the next Sunday. It said, *Tim at Talladega.*

He wondered what he would do if given the choice between running away with his real mother or staying with the Maxwells. They weren't perfect, but they cared. They took him away from Tyson and Vera. But no matter how many good things they did, they weren't his own flesh and blood.

He put the mail on the desk and went to his room.

Chapter 20
Onto the Track

JAMIE'S DAD QUALIFIED the #14 car in ninth position for the race. Devalon was behind him in the 15th spot and not too happy about it. Her dad had repeatedly tried to talk with Devalon before the race and had even tried to get a message to him through Devalon's teammate, but it was no use.

At the chapel service before the race, the chaplain continued what he called his Chase Series about people in the Bible God had used to do great things. At New Hampshire he had talked about Jonah, at Dover he went over Noah's life, and at Kansas he highlighted Abraham.

"All of these people had messed up their lives terribly, but God looked at their faith in him. For example, it says that 'even when there was no reason for hope, Abraham kept hoping.' Now this wasn't blind hope that some people have—like I hope I'm going to get skinny even though I'm eating four double cheeseburgers and a large french fry. God had told Abraham that he would become the father of many nations, and even though he and his wife were old, he believed what God had told him. He believed the words God had spoken to him, and he wouldn't back down."

Jamie thought more about that as the race was about to begin. How much did she believe God was guiding her? How much did she want to just control things by herself? If God was giving the green flag to racing, would he just plop her into a car, or would she have to work on it as hard, if not harder?

That was going through her mind when the call came: "Gentlemen, start your engines." *They'll have to change that gentlemen thing in a couple of years when I'm racing,* she thought. She looked at her watch—2:12 p.m.

The green flag dropped at the speedway, and the field shot through the first turn. She adjusted her headset to listen to her dad and tuned in the announcers by mistake.

". . . and there is some increasing animosity between the #13 and #14 teams of Butch Devalon and Dale Maxwell," the announcer said. "We'll watch how the race heats up to see if the conflict spills onto the track, but there was a fire this week at the Devalon garage that was deliberately set, and Butch blames a young man who lives with Maxwell and his family."

"Something tells me that's not the only thing those two are fighting over," a commentator said. "They're battling it out for the play-offs of NASCAR and neither one of them wants to lose."

"This, of course, would be Butch Devalon's third cup championship. Dale Maxwell has never been—"

"Oh, did you see that?" another commentator, a former crew chief, said. "Devalon just moved up a couple of spots and got right behind Dale and stole some air from him—got him loose."

"There's no love lost there, but I'm surprised it happened this early in the race."

Jamie quickly tuned to her dad's channel.

"Just keep your cool. Nobody got hurt," T.J. said.

"Yeah, but we lost our position," her dad said. "You know he did that on purpose."

"The officials will be watching to see if you give him payback," T.J. said. "Keep it clean out there. We've got more than 250 laps left. Plenty of time to show what you're made of."

"I'll keep it clean. I'm just going to hunt him down and pass him."

Jamie smiled as she watched her dad zoom back

into the field. He was now in 25th place while Devalon had already made his move into the top 10.

After a caution from a car into the wall on lap 20, the restart showed seven of the chasers in the top 10. Jamie's dad was in the 19th spot and moving up. Then, on the 85th lap, a slower car being lapped veered left toward the pits and tagged the #01 car, one of the top contenders in the Chase, and sent him spinning. The #01 car tried to stay out of the pits but began smoking with a tire rub and had to come in.

The race announcers talked to him in his headset.

"This is what happens when you've got guys trying to make it to the top, and there are some others with less experience out here," the #01 driver said. "It makes it exciting for the fans, but it can be frustrating here on the track."

Jamie thought it was a tactful way of saying he was spitting mad at the younger driver.

"We've got to get you up front into the lead for a few laps," T.J. said to her dad. "If you don't, even if you win, we'll be behind."

"Hey, if I get to the front, I don't want to lead for just a few laps," her dad said.

"Ten-four," T.J. said.

On lap 115, with everyone coming in during a caution, Jamie's dad was in 15th place and decided to take just two tires. It was a risky move, but he got off pit road in the third spot. When the race resumed, he challenged the #51 car and took the lead on lap 124. At the restart, six of the top 10 drivers were chasers.

"Feels good up front in the clean Kansas air," her dad said.

"Number 13 coming up fast," Scotty radioed her dad.

"Kinda figured that would happen," her dad said.

Her dad had led 10 laps, picking up extra points, when Butch Devalon challenged. Jamie saw the familiar black Chevy moving up in the monitors. She knew her dad was no match for Devalon and his four fresh tires, but he kept the inside line and made Devalon pass him on the outside. For two more laps her dad battled with him, struggling to keep the lead. Finally Devalon passed him (or her dad let him) and took over first. Jamie was just glad Devalon didn't try to crash her dad.

"I'm wearing out my tires and brakes out here," her dad said.

A few laps later there was another caution for debris on the track, and her dad came in for two more tires. He dropped out of the top 10 but was in a good position for the race.

A blown engine in the middle of the pack sent four cars to the garage on lap 180. At that point, Devalon was leading the field by nearly half a second and had led more than 60 laps of the race.

"We gotta get back up front, Dale. There's no two ways about it," T.J. said.

At the restart, her dad was in 11th place, with less than 70 laps to go. Jamie knew if he wanted to contend seriously for the championship, he'd need to at least finish in the top 10.

"We have a window here between lap 220 and 230, Dale," T.J. said. "You're good on fuel, but you're going to need new tires."

"All right, let me get back to you."

While Jamie watched her dad on the in-car camera, the team's public relations representative, Chloe Snowe, came up behind her. Chloe was dating Billy Reuters, driver of the #72 car, and there were rumors of an engagement. She had silky blonde hair and a beauty pageant figure (because she'd been Miss Mississippi), but all the guys on the team knew there was more to her than a pretty face. She had made changes to the way they communicated with the media and had gotten several stories advanced about Jamie's dad, putting him in the spotlight and helping calm the sponsors' nerves.

"What's he doing in there?" Chloe said, squinting at the screen. "Looks like he's talking to somebody, but I don't hear anything on the radio."

"He is talking to somebody," Jamie said. "God."

Chloe raised her eyebrows. "I know he takes his faith seriously, but what's he praying about?"

"He told me there are times when he doesn't know what to do during a race, and he'll just ask God for wisdom."

Chloe looked like she'd tasted a lemon. "Does he ever hear anything?"

"I think he does most of the talking," Jamie said, smiling. "He said he's never heard a voice, but sometimes something will come to mind, you know, triggering another race, another similar situation, and he'll go with it."

Chloe stared at the screen. "Well, I hope he gets a strong feeling about this one."

Chapter 21
Last Laps

TIM PACED in front of the TV in the living room while Kellen sat on the couch eating Crunch 'n Munch. Mrs. Maxwell had gone to the church to watch the race with friends. There simply wasn't enough room in their house to hold all the people interested, but Tim could tell that she didn't really want to go. She probably wanted to stay home with them but felt like she should at least show up.

"I'll be back here to watch the finish," she had said.

Tim couldn't remember being this caught up in the racing season. He had rooted for the driver his dad worked for, but it always seemed like a business back then. Get to the track, get qualified, try not to get a DNF, and move on to the next race. Now it felt fresh and new and like there was a point to all the weekly madness. And he was surprised how much he wanted Dale to win.

"I can't believe he's really got a shot at the championship," Kellen said, a big piece of popcorn sticking to one cheek. Kellen's mouth was full, so it came out sounding like, "I mmf bemmf hmff remmfffy gaat a shmmt at the chammffionffff."

A car pulled up outside as one of the commentators, a former racer himself, said, "Here come the leaders into the pits for their final stop. The finish of the race may depend on this stop and how fast—"

"Whoa!" the announcer interrupted. "Dale Maxwell looked like he was about to pit, but he pulled off the apron and back onto the track while every other leader gets fuel and new tires."

"He's pulling a Phoenix," Kellen said, dropping the box to the floor. The door opened and Mrs. Maxwell ran in. "Dad's doing a Phoenix. He just faked them out and stayed off pit road."

Mrs. Maxwell's mouth dropped open, and she sat in the big cushy chair near the TV.

"What's a Phoenix?" Tim said.

"In a cup race in his first season he was second about 30 laps from finishing. He acted like he was going to pit, then jumped back on the track and everybody else had to pit."

"What happened?" Tim said.

"He led for about 10 laps," Mrs. Maxwell said, her eyes still glued to the TV. "Then he lost a left front tire on the back straightaway. Finished 15th."

"Were you there?" Tim said.

"I went to all of the races before we had kids," she said. "We were full-time on the road."

"Which do you like better?" Tim said.

She smiled. "I don't have to sit in the pits to be with him."

The screen showed Dale on the in-camera, talking with his crew chief. Then came a split screen of Dale and T.J. Kelly talking, and it was clear there was a difference of opinion.

"Dale, there's no way you're going to finish on those tires," T.J. said. "And you're maybe a lap or two from seeing them give out on you."

"I gotcha. Just need to stay out here a few more laps."

Pit road emptied, and the other cars tried to catch up with him. The camera showed a problem on pit road with Butch Devalon's team. The jack failed and they had to use a backup, but that took precious seconds from him. It was clear he was mad as he banged on the steering wheel. The TV coverage didn't air his audio, but Tim could tell it wasn't appropriate for a family audience.

Mrs. Maxwell put her head in her hands, and it looked like she was praying.

"This looks good for Dale now," the former racer said, "but I've gotta tell you, with the race on the line and the Chase on the line, this is one risky move. He blows a tire out there, and at best he could fight just to get back to his pit stall—worst case, he slams into the wall and doesn't even finish."

"You would have played it differently?" the announcer said.

"You bet. He's in contention for the championship, and the worst thing you could do here is take a risk to win something and not finish. The cars behind him have fresh tires, and they're already making up time."

"Well, he's not listening to you."

"He's not listening to his crew chief either. Listen to this exchange on that last lap."

"Dale, you need new tires," T.J. said in what Tim thought was as much of a pleading voice as he'd ever heard on an exchange between crew chief and driver. "There's no way around it. We're past our window, and you'll run out of fuel within five laps. Six tops."

"Ten-four," Dale said.

They showed another shot of Dale in the cockpit bearing down on a lapped car. He looked to Tim like a guy sure of himself. Tim couldn't see Dale's face through that helmet and visor, but he imagined a smile there.

"There are 32 laps left here at the Kansas Speedway," the announcer said. "Can Dale Maxwell keep this lead on little fuel and no tires? We'll find out when we return."

The coverage cut away to a commercial, and Mrs. Maxwell told Kellen to turn down the volume. She had her eyes closed and her lips were moving. Kellen closed his eyes too, and Tim couldn't help but smile because there was still some Crunch 'n Munch on his face.

"Father, in the whole scheme of things a NASCAR race doesn't mean that much," Mrs. Maxwell prayed. "But you know how important this is to Dale and what he wants to accomplish for you. I pray you'll give him wisdom that can come only from you. Show him *your* path and help him follow it no matter what."

"And help him stay in front of Devalon, Lord," Kellen prayed.

As they ping-ponged back and forth, Tim watched the commercials, thinking at any minute they'd break back into the coverage and show Dale's tire flopping on the side of the car like a fish in the bottom of a bass boat.

"No matter what happens, help him to give glory to you," Mrs. Maxwell finished. As soon as she opened her eyes, the screen went black and the coverage of the race continued.

The first image shown was the #14 car of Dale Maxwell speeding past the start/finish line, no competitor within 20 car lengths of him. Instead of being caught, he'd actually extended his lead. The shot switched to the camera on the blimp above, showing the gap.

"Only 25 laps left in this race and Dale Maxwell still leads here in Kansas," the announcer said, "and T.J. Kelly sounds desperate over there in the war wagon."

They cut to the on-track reporter. "What's going on out there between you and Dale?" She stuck a microphone in T.J.'s face.

"Sometimes drivers can be stubborn," T.J. said, shaking his head, half smiling.

"How much fuel does he have left?"

"He should have run out a lap ago. Running on fumes."

"And his tires?"

"You couldn't use the rubber on those tires to make a tennis ball," T.J. said.

"Trouble in turn four!" a commentator shouted.

The shot switched to the final turn, where three cars had crashed. It was a bad wreck, with twisted metal and one front end smashed halfway to the cockpit.

"I cannot believe this, boys," the commentator

said. "They're going to have to bring the field down pit road and . . . yeah, we're getting the word now the pits will be open in one lap. Let's see if Dale can make it around one more time before that car stops or falls apart."

Mrs. Maxwell was on her feet, both hands behind her head, and Kellen was whooping and yelling. Tim couldn't hold in his excitement, which came out as a chuckle that turned into a laugh.

Dale made it all the way around to pit road before he ran out of gas. "T.J., I'm coasting your way."

He pulled in, and the crew went to work putting on four new tires and filling his tank with enough fuel for the final laps. The car didn't fire the first time, and Tim's heart sank. Then it came to life as the jack let the left side down, and Dale screamed out of his stall, every member of the crew pumping their fists in the air.

"Looks like Dale is going to make it first off pit road," the commentator said. "His gamble has paid off so far. Now let's see if he can finish this thing."

Chapter 22
Finish Line

JAMIE WENT OVER to take a look at the tires they'd pulled off her dad's car. When the torch hit the rubber, it melted straight through. A camera crew came over and shot the second tire, which did the same thing. Jamie could imagine what the guys in the booth were saying. There was just nothing left of these tires.

She turned her attention to the track. The debris was almost cleared. When the restart came there would be about 15 laps left. Her dad was in first place, but the Chase drivers were now bunched up right behind him. Butch Devalon had overcome the mishap with the jack and was back in third place.

Someone tapped her on the shoulder; it was the on-track reporter. He handed her a pair of headphones with a microphone attached and pointed at the grandstand—as if telling her someone wanted to talk to her.

"Jamie, this is Jack in the booth. You got a good look at those tires. What do you think?"

"They aren't tires anymore," Jamie said. "Just big hunks of rubber."

"If you could have been up on that war wagon, what would you have told him?"

Jamie laughed. "You don't tell my dad anything. When he gets it in his head he's right, you stand back and try to stay out of his way."

"Can you believe what's happened this season?" the announcer said. "To have the year start so badly and then turn it around?"

"Well, it just shows you have to stay behind the wheel and keep the tires spinning. You can't give up because things are going badly. Good things can happen with a little momentum."

"Hey, thanks, Jamie."

Jamie was about to take off the headset when she heard, "She's a chip off the old block, isn't she?"

"Yeah, and the way she drove in Denver, it wouldn't surprise me to see her out here herself in the next couple of years."

The reporter and camera guy moved on, and Jamie went back to the war wagon and found Chloe in front of the monitor. The pit crew was crowded around behind her. The jackman was the only one not watching—he was sitting on a stack of tires looking exhausted. He gave Jamie a weak thumbs-up and stood.

"You okay?" Jamie said.

He nodded. "If your dad wins this thing, I'm gonna quit."

"What? Are you serious?"

He smiled. "I'll quit because I've just experienced the most incredible thing I've ever seen."

They walked to the wall and watched as the green flag came out. It was a single-file restart, and her dad punched the throttle right before the line and got at least a three-car-length lead. Jamie focused on Butch Devalon in third place as he struggled to pass the car in front of him so he could get at her dad.

The next 12 laps felt like 100 to Jamie as the cars screamed around the track. She waited for a crash that would bunch the cars up and set up a shoot-out, but the race stayed clean.

Butch Devalon finally pulled into second place, but the closest he could get was about a car length away, and then her dad pulled away again and won the race.

The crew went wild, and T.J. slapped high fives all around and patted people on the back.

When Jamie's dad pulled into the winner's circle,

the crowd cheered and the team stood around the car and shook one of the sponsor's sodas all over her dad. He climbed out and acknowledged the crowd. Jamie stood behind the car and watched. She was crying she was so happy. The reporter asked what was going through his mind and stuck the microphone in front of him.

"I have to thank my wife and family for sticking so tight with me through a lot of years. Nicole, Kellen, and where's Jamie? Come over here. And, Tim, this is for you too, buddy. And to the giver of all good things I'm thankful today. This was a great race, and I thank the sponsors who hung in there with me. . . ."

Her dad named all the sponsors, and then the reporter took the mike back. "Tell us what happened out there when you didn't pit but stayed on the track. T.J. Kelly was pleading with you to come in."

"I know T.J. wanted to win as badly as I did, but I felt like we should stay out and fight through it. I couldn't begin to explain it, but I just knew in my gut that we'd be okay."

Jamie's dad hugged her, and she got to experience the winner's circle like never before. He held up the trophy above his head, and the crowd cheered more.

A few Devalon fans booed next to the fence and yelled, "You're washed up, Maxwell!"

Her dad smiled and didn't respond.

As they walked back to the hauler, Jamie noticed something running down her dad's face. "You still sweating, or are those tears?"

He smiled, and his skin crinkled with those familiar lines. He stopped and looked at the stands emptying. There were still many people there, and he pointed at them. "Winning feels so good. But you know what I really want?"

"You just won the race. You're fifth in the Chase. What more could you want? The championship?"

He shook his head. "Something's been burning deep down inside me for a long time. There's a lot of people up there who know all about racing but next to nothing about God and how much he loves them. I think the Lord wants me to be bolder with my witness to them. I think he wants to use me in a greater way."

"What does that mean?"

Her dad shook his head. "I'm not sure. I just know I need to seize the opportunities I have when they come."

When they were back at the hauler, after everybody had patted her dad on the back and told him what a great race he had run, Jamie pulled him aside. "All right, fess up. Why did you stay out there that long? Why didn't you come in when T.J. told you to?"

T.J. walked in just then with a worried look on his face. "I'd like to hear the answer to that too. You took an awful big chance out there, Dale. I know you won, and I'm happy for us, but this can destroy our confidence if you don't listen to what we say."

Her dad put a hand on T.J.'s shoulder. Touching people was his way of connecting. "I was listening to you. I didn't dismiss your call."

"Then why didn't you come in?" T.J. said, almost shouting.

"Because I heard something I couldn't ignore."

T.J. closed his eyes. "God's not talking to you now, is he? I mean, I know you talk to him throughout the race, but . . ."

Jamie's dad smiled. "I didn't hear any voices, no. But I knew I was supposed to stay out there and get the lead. I've never had it happen that strongly. And I'm sorry you felt like I was ignoring you. I really am. I just wouldn't have been able to live with myself if I hadn't listened to what I was hearing."

T.J. nodded. "I understand." He reached out a hand and shook her dad's. "It's been good working with you. But I think this is our last race together."

"What?" Jamie said.

T.J. shook his head. "We've got a great chance to do something special. But if you're not going to listen to us and if you're going to follow the voices in your head or what you think is right, then there's no reason for me to be on that wagon."

Scotty walked in and piled his radio equipment on the counter. "I feel the same way, Dale. If you'd have tried to go around one more lap, we'd have been at the back of the pack. We'd have lost and you'd be pretty far back in the Chase."

Her dad rubbed his chin. "Look. You two are right. We race as a team, and the crew chief is the quarterback. I was the running back here looking at an open field, and I called an audible. I'll try not to do that again."

"You'll try?" T.J. said. "That's not good enough. I know you own this car. You pay our salaries. *You're* the quarterback. But when you go off and do something like you did today, it means all of us could lose."

"But we won," Jamie said, coming to her dad's defense. "If he'd have pitted when you wanted him to, he wouldn't have won the race and you know it."

T.J. sighed. "We'll never know that. And you're right, we did win. But look how close we came to losing it all."

Scotty pointed at Jamie. "Let's say you're the crew chief, Dale, and you know Jamie needs to come in for fresh tires and fuel. You tell her to but she doesn't. What would you do?"

"I'd chew her out good when she blew a tire," her dad said.

"Exactly," Scotty said. "You wouldn't want *her* doing what you did out there."

Her dad nodded. "In all the races we've been through together, there's probably a handful where I've done this, right?"

T.J. and Scotty nodded.

"Then trust me when I say I won't do it again. If we disagree, I'll give you every chance to talk me out of it. We're a team here. We just won a huge race, and we've got seven more."

There was an awkward silence between them.

Finally T.J. put out a hand. "I guess if it means a championship, I can't walk away from that."

Scotty put his hand over T.J.'s. "It's hard to walk away from a winner."

Jamie put her hand in, and her dad put his on top of it.

"Let's show them what a great team can do," he said.

Chapter 23
Tim at Talladega

TIM WAS HOPING that Butch Devalon would have a heart and retract his ban on his being in the pits, but after the results of Kansas, Devalon was even madder at the Maxwells and wouldn't even return phone calls. The police still hadn't officially cleared Tim about the fire, which troubled him. Dale had said they would issue some kind of statement about his innocence soon, but the whole thing hung over him at school. Lots of people had heard he was a suspect, and he felt their stares as he walked into class.

The week dragged, and Tim lost himself in the NASCAR talk shows. People called to talk about the Devalon/Maxwell feud. Some backed Dale, others Devalon, and some just thought the grudge brought a level of excitement that the sport needed.

A major magazine (not NASCAR) put Dale and Butch on its cover with a big headline that said, "Good Guy vs. Bad Guy." They used parts of the Calvin Shoverton article in the coverage. Tim couldn't believe some of Devalon's quotes. One said, "I'm painted as this bad driver who wrecks people and doesn't care. That's not true. I just want to win. I care a lot about people. Look at how much of my winnings go to charity."

Tim rolled his eyes when he read that. Everybody knew the drivers gave to charity because it was good PR plus a good idea to avoid higher taxes. As far as Tim could tell, the Maxwells gave a lot of their money to their church and some select charities. They didn't talk about it much, but once Tim had found their checkbook out on the kitchen table and caught sight of a couple of checks they'd written.

Dale was gone a couple of days running tests for the upcoming races and doing some more media and a commercial for one of the sponsors. The phone rang just about constantly, and Tim got so fed up with it that he turned the ringer off on the one in his room.

Mrs. Maxwell drove him, Jamie, and Kellen to Talladega on Saturday. They stayed at a hotel with a *suites* in its name that was a long way from the superspeedway. Dale joined them for dinner, and they ate at a nice steak place and got a special booth in the back, where they wouldn't be bothered by people who recognized Dale. Tim ordered surf and turf, which was some shrimp and a hunk of steak, plus french-fried onion rings and mashed potatoes that looked like he could eat them for dessert. It was more food than he could possibly finish, so he took it back to the room and put it in the little refrigerator, along with a piece of strawberry cheesecake that probably had enough calories in it to keep him going for a month.

He was munching on the onion rings, watching an old James Bond movie with Kellen, when Dale came in and turned the volume down just as one of the bad guys was being pushed out of a plane.

"Got some good news," Dale said, sitting on the edge of one of the beds. "You're going to be down in the pits tomorrow."

Tim did a double take. "You serious?"

"You bet," Dale said. "Devalon is still making a stink about it and probably will through the whole race, but the people at the track overruled him. They remember what happened here last year, and they said they didn't care if you burned down half of North Carolina—they weren't going to be the ones to keep you out."

Tim smiled. "There are some good people here."

Dale nodded. "I don't suppose I have to tell you to be on your best behavior and that everybody's going to be watching."

"No. I'll be a little angel."

"That'll be the day." Kellen laughed.

"We got an early day tomorrow," Dale said. "You two get some rest. We have to be at the track before the rush."

/////

It was a foreign thing for Tim to drive to a race—with his dad, he had always slept either at the track or in a nearby fleabag hotel. The family got up, ate breakfast in the restaurant downstairs, packed their stuff, and headed for the track. A few miles later they hit traffic, and it was stop-and-go until they got to the gate.

The guy at the front looked inside, saw everyone, and tipped his hat. "Nice to have you here, Mrs. Maxwell." He pointed out where they could park, but Mrs. Maxwell acted like she'd been to the track a hundred times.

The RVs and campers were just starting to stir. Saturday night was the rowdiest night of Talladega. A lot of people came early in the week and stayed to party, and the race signaled the end. Tim's dad had always kept him away from that scene, but he couldn't help hearing the music and smelling the food cooking on grills. Even now there were people out cooking sausages for breakfast, wearing their favorite drivers' hats and T-shirts.

They found the Maxwell hauler and put their stuff inside, then wandered over to the garage. Fans already milled around, trying to get an autograph or a picture with some famous driver. Tim figured a lot of people would probably think it boring to just stand around watching people working on cars, but he found it fascinating. There was always something to learn about the way someone approached an engine, what they looked for when they heard a noise, what the driver felt when he sensed a particular movement or heard something out of the ordinary.

A little later Dale came by, and they had lunch at the hauler under one of the tents set up to keep the sun from baking them like the bratwurst and onions and hot dogs on the grill. Dale ate some pasta and stuff that would stick with him through the race. There was the old air of excitement, food, fuel smell, heat rising from the concrete, and nerves of the crew. In one way, it was a lot easier not to be in the Chase. You didn't have the pressure of worrying about a lug nut going on crooked or being the goat who messed up the pit stop. Most of the guys played it cool, pretending to relax and even sleeping, but Tim knew that they were eating Rolaids like they were candy.

After the drivers' meeting, the chaplain stood and prepared for the chapel service. Most of the drivers scampered out like someone had dropped a skunk under their chairs. The guy was doing a series on people in the Bible God had chased or something like that, but Tim found it hard to concentrate with the excitement of the race just ahead. He couldn't understand how Dale or any of the other drivers and crew members could focus on God stuff when they were about to do the most thrilling thing in their lives. Jamie and Mrs. Maxwell were glued to every word.

Tim closed his eyes at the end but just so he could rest them. Getting up early each day for school exhausted him, and on the weekend he liked to sleep in. Traveling and getting up early this morning had caught up with him.

They walked back to the hauler and met a family with a little girl Tim thought looked familiar. Her name was Jenna, and all three of them looked like it was Christmas morning they were so excited.

"I saw you at that camp, didn't I?" Tim said to Jenna.

"Yeah, I've got diabetes," Jenna said, "and Mr. Maxwell said if he made it in the Chase, he'd pay for us to come here."

"Well, you are his good luck charm," Tim said. "He should have done that a long time ago."

"Excuse me," she said, "but I don't believe in luck. God works in our lives and nothing happens by chance."

Her mom and dad smiled, and Tim nodded. He wanted to ask her, *So, did he give you diabetes?*

"I know what you're thinking," Jenna said. "You're thinking, 'Did God give me diabetes?'"

Tim's eyes widened. "Well, as a matter of fact . . ."

She kept talking as they walked through the hauler. "I don't think God *gave* me diabetes to punish me or because he doesn't like me. He allows different hard things to help his children grow. You know, like a farmer pruning his trees."

"So he did make you have diabetes," Tim said.

"It's impossible to understand it all because we're just puny little humans. But the way I look at it, God let us choose whether to follow him or not, and sin came into the world. After that came diseases and all kinds of bad stuff. God didn't cause that to happen, but since he was in control, he allowed it to happen."

"So you don't blame him?"

"How could I be mad at somebody who died for me? He loves me. And he's given me not one but two pancreases to take care of me." Jenna explained that her parents acted as her pancreas, giving her insulin every day.

Dale took them to the pits and showed them the car. After that it was time to get ready. Jenna and her family stood back and put on their headphones.

Dale turned to Tim. "You ready for this?"

Tim looked around. "Is Devalon gonna sneak up and attack me?"

Dale laughed. "No. Just wait a minute."

After the introduction of the drivers, the announcer asked people to stand and remove their hats. Then a picture of Tim's dad flashed on live television. "One year ago, Martin Carhardt tragically lost his life here at Talladega. Joining us today with the Dale Maxwell team is his son, Tim Carhardt."

Tim was stunned by the announcement and was even more surprised when *his* face flashed on the screen.

Before the announcer could continue, the crowd applauded and cheered.

Tim couldn't help smiling, and he dipped his head and looked at the ground.

Finally the announcer went on. "In tribute to this fallen friend, we ask for a moment of silence in his memory, after which we'll hear the prayer from NASCAR's chaplain."

The stands fell silent—an eerie sound for a place that made so much noise. A few seconds later, someone yelled, "We love you, Tim!"

Then the chaplain prayed, a singer performed the national anthem, and jets flew overhead.

Dale pounded Tim on the back. "Didn't expect that, did you?"

Tim shook his head. "It was nice. Thanks for setting that up."

"I didn't have anything to do with it," Dale said. "They did that on their own."

Tim nodded. "Well, I thank you anyway."

Dale's pit box was close to the end of pit road this year, which made Tim glad. He stood back as Mrs. Maxwell handed Dale a slip of paper. Tim guessed it was the verse she gave him before each race (or read to him over the phone when she wasn't there in person). He didn't have the nerve to ask what it said. Dale kissed her, then got in the car and strapped in, and the chaplain came along and prayed with him.

Then the call came—"Gentlemen, start your engines!"

Tim loved the sound of the engines together, and when the cars pulled in behind the pace car, he couldn't believe the noise and the power of those engines. And that was before they actually started racing!

"You okay?" Jamie said to him.

"Yeah, I'm good."

"Did it bring back some bad memories?" she said.

"A little," Tim said. "But there's so much good I remember about my dad that I don't think about this track as being the problem. I'm kind of glad to be back here."

Jamie walked a little farther down pit road with her headset on, and Tim turned to the race. Dale started in the 12th position, and when the green flag waved, he and the others shot forward, drafting in two long trains.

Chapter 24
Air Box

IT TOOK ALL Jamie had to talk with Tim. He looked so alone up on the screen, and he looked even more forlorn standing near the wall. After she spoke to him, she had to walk away because her eyes filled.

The Talladega track was huge—a 2.66-mile tri-oval—with seats for nearly 150,000 and enough camping for thousands more. The grounds were a living, moving organism that came alive during race week, and as the Chase unfolded, Jamie couldn't help but picture herself racing here, taking the lead on the straightaway and leading one of the trains.

Her dad had explained drafting to her when she was little and even showed her what it felt like by driving close to an 18-wheeler on the interstate, but there was no way she could understand it until she saw it up close. A car going at such a high speed would be sucked into the air of another car in front of it and propelled around the track. It was discovered in the late 1950s at Daytona when a driver followed other cars around the track, using their speed to make him go faster. He won the race and the secret was out.

"I got a problem," Jamie's dad said on the radio. "Air box is gone."

T.J. went back and forth with him about the box, but it was clear it wasn't working.

Kellen came up behind her. "What happens if he doesn't have an air box?"

"That's the way he stays cool," Jamie yelled. "He loses that and he'll cook inside there for 500 miles."

"I'm real sorry about that, Dale," T.J. radioed back. "From what we can tell, the wires are fried in the box. You're just going to have to tough it out."

"Can't he get some air through the window?" Kellen said.

"Going that fast, you don't get any air at all," Jamie said.

"Looks like I'm going to lose a little weight in here," Dale said.

Jamie shook her head. It was a blistering day in Alabama. Her dad was tough, but enough laps driving in 130-degree heat and it would begin working on his brain. Fatigue would set in. *There has to be something we can do,* she thought.

She turned to look for Tim, but he wasn't near the pits. "Where did Tim go?" she said to Kellen.

He shrugged. "Wasn't my day to watch him."

The #14 car was in the middle of a pack of cars going three wide when her dad spoke again. "I feel like a turkey on Thanksgiving Day. T.J., you gotta check this thing next time before the race. How did it get past you?"

She could count on the fingers of one hand the number of times her dad had spoken harshly on the radio. It was clear he was in a difficult situation that was only going to get worse as the day wore on.

"I'm real sorry about that," T.J. said. "I feel your pain."

"First pit stop, I want a bucket of ice dumped in here. You got me?"

T.J. laughed. "Maybe I can just get you a Coca-Cola truck to drive. That'd be a lot cooler."

"I'm serious," Dale said. "I've eaten cooked ham that's cooler than I am right now."

Jamie watched her dad. He was keeping pace with all the other drivers. He had to because if he slowed down, he'd cause a wreck. Out of the corner of her eye she saw Tim running from the garage to the war wagon. He was carrying something and timidly looking up at T.J.

Chapter 25
Tim's Idea

TIM FINALLY GOT T.J.'S ATTENTION.

T.J. took a headphone off one ear and leaned down. "What is it?"

"I've got this hose I rigged up from stuff in the hauler," Tim said. "If we hook it to the window net and snake the tube in, you can at least get some air into Dale's helmet."

T.J. leaned down a little farther, and Tim handed him the contraption. It was made out of a piece of plastic tubing connected to a funnel. Tim had made sure it was a new one so it wouldn't give Dale any fumes. He also fastened two metal clips through the plastic that would hold it securely to the netting and withstand the extreme wind velocity.

"Take this to the extra man," T.J. said, pointing to him. He got on the radio. "Dale, Tim has come up with something we'll try on the next pit stop.

I need to make sure the officials will let us use our extra man. It'll fasten onto the window net, and you'll get some air if you fit it up inside your suit."

"Ten-four," Dale said.

T.J. contacted the NASCAR official and asked permission to have the extra man go over the wall. Occasionally an eighth man was allowed to clean the windshield or help the driver. The permission came, but unfortunately for Dale there was plenty of green-flag racing ahead. He didn't come in for a tire change until lap 37, and it was under green.

The extra man went over the wall. He stuck the hose inside, and Dale helped secure the clips perfectly to the netting. It was on only a couple of seconds when the left side came down and Dale screamed away from the pits, trying to get back to the field without going down a lap.

"Watch your speed," T.J. said.

Dale returned to the race and radioed a lap later. "I'm as cool as a cucumber in here. Tim ought to patent this thing for all the drivers who have air boxes go down."

Tim couldn't help smiling.

As the race continued, the anticipation from the fans rose about "the big one," the normal crash everyone had become accustomed to at Talladega. At some point in the 500-mile race, with cars going at incredible speeds and incredibly close together, someone made a mistake, had a blowout, or got loose in a turn, and several cars were taken out.

About halfway through, Dale was in a line of cars drafting on the inside. Another line had formed beside them, and like two 10-car trains, they rumbled down the track. As they approached turn one, Tim noticed the second car in Dale's line get loose and spin into the line beside them.

The crowd gasped and people rose to their feet. Tim strained to see through the smoke and debris. It was only a split second, but it felt like an hour.

"Stay low. Stay low. Stay low," Scotty said on the radio.

The #14 car finally emerged on the other side of the wreck.

"Good job," Scotty said.

In all, five cars had to leave the race, and four more had to go back to the garage and would return later.

"That was a close one," Dale said.

"Good job staying clear," T.J. said. "You're in 12th position as it stands now, and when they clean these cars up, you may be even higher."

T.J. was right. Though Dale's engine showed signs of running hot, a blistering-fast pit stop helped (they pulled the grille tape to help cool it off), and he moved into the top 10. There had been a number of lead changes, but Butch Devalon was on top now and leading the pack at the bottom of the track.

At lap 166, T.J. came on the radio. “Unless you’re hearing voices about what to do, we’re going to be out of fuel soon.”

“Yeah, I’m thinking I need to come in for just fuel.”

“You sure you don’t want right-side tires?” T.J. said.

“No, they’re good. Let’s come in for enough to get us to the finish.”

“You got it,” T.J. said.

Chapter 26
Fire

JAMIE GAVE A SIGH of relief when her dad got back onto the track after a fuel stop. There were several cars out of the race now, and 24 were on the lead lap. After a yellow flag for debris, all 24 started single file with Butch Devalon in the lead. Her dad had pulled out of line to pass earlier, and the wind resistance sent him back to 15th place.

"Thought I was going to get a push back there from the #51," her dad said on the radio.

"We'll get it back," T.J. said. "Don't try to be a hero out there. Let's get a good finish."

Come on, Dad, Jamie thought. Sometimes he did things she didn't understand. That move was a mistake a rookie would make. He'd seen an opening and moved out, not counting on the wind pushing him toward the back of the pack.

Butch Devalon led them to the restart at lap 180, with just nine laps to go. At lap 183, three cars finally got out of line, trying to pass Devalon. Her dad moved out of line again, creating a middle lane, but this time four cars followed him. They were three wide now, and her dad was being pushed to the front, right next to Devalon and the line of cars on the outside.

In turn four, the #16 car, the leader of the outside lane, zoomed ahead and took over the lead from Devalon, but neither Devalon nor her dad was giving up easy. Still three wide, #16 cut to the middle lane right in front of her dad.

Jamie switched to the network coverage and found the announcer going crazy. "This is going to be an incredible finish," he said. "The 24 cars on the lead lap are less than 1.5 seconds apart."

"And all 12 Chase contenders are right in there hoping they can get more points," a commentator said.

"Here comes Butch Devalon pushing ahead on the inside now to retake the lead."

"He's not giving up."

"No, he's not, and neither is the #16 and the #14 right beside him."

"You can bet Dale Maxwell is trying his best to push them forward so he can move over ahead of Devalon and get a push from him."

"With all that's been going on between those two, he's likely to get more than a push."

Jamie laughed and looked at Tim, who was into the race. He was leaning against the wall near the Maxwell team, watching intently. Her mom was on the war wagon, standing by the railing with Kellen right next to her, his hands balled into fists.

"Whoa," the announcer said.

"Trouble!" another said.

"There's smoke coming from the #33 engine on the outside, and the caution flag comes out here on lap 186. What a bad break for that team here at the end of the 500 miles."

"Looks like we'll get a green-white-checkered."

Jamie paced near the team. Her dad didn't need more fuel. His tires were iffy. A few cars hit pit road, but the leaders stayed out, including her dad. When the green flag waved on lap 191, there were two laps to go. Her dad was on the outside, second car in line. Devalon led on the inside.

The white flag flew, and as far as Jamie could tell, her dad was in third place—until the middle lane opened up and two team members came from the high side, followed by four other cars. On the back straightaway they were three wide.

Every person in the stands and on the infield was on their feet, yelling. Jamie ran to the wall to see the finish for herself. As she passed the war wagon there was a screech of metal and smoke. She glanced at the monitor where Chloe Snowe stood.

"Field's frozen," she said.

"Where's Dad?" Jamie said as cars passed the start line.

"I think he was fifth when it was frozen—"

"No, I mean where is he now?" Jamie interrupted.

Chloe looked back at the track, then at the screen. "He's at the bottom of the track. He's getting out of his car."

The replay showed that the #21 car had hit the wall hard and flipped over, scraping its top and coming down the track. On its way, two cars had crashed into it, making the flames worse.

When the TV coverage cut live to the track, her dad was at the #21 car's window, pulling the net down, waving at the emergency crew. He jumped back as a flame burst out the window. Then dived back in. Seconds later he pulled the driver out of the window and dragged him away from the car.

/////

Tim stood outside the infield care center with the rest of the Maxwell family and a gaggle of reporters and cameras. Dale finally came out with a bandage over one eye. His eyebrows had been singed, and there was also a bandage on one arm. Before he answered any questions, he hugged and kissed Mrs. Maxwell. Jamie and Kellen hugged him too.

"Dale, describe what happened out there," a reporter said.

"Well, I haven't seen the replay, but I saw Jimmy hit hard into the wall above me, and the #18 got into me from below and I drifted down. When everybody got past, I saw the fire and that Jimmy wasn't moving, so I ran over there."

"Do you have any injuries?"

"Just burned my eyebrows a little. It wasn't anything big."

"And what about Jimmy?"

"He was knocked out for a few minutes. I heard him talking when they got him to the care center, though. First time I was ever glad to hear Jimmy talking."

Everybody laughed nervously.

"You knew the field had been frozen when you climbed out of your car, right?" the reporter said.

Dale snickered. "At that point you don't care who froze what or whether you come in third or 43rd. You just want to get your friend out of harm's way."

"You finished seventh. How do you feel about your chances for the rest of the Chase?"

"I feel pretty good. We seem to be getting stronger as the season goes on, which is the way you want it. If I can run like we did today the rest of the season, we'll be in good shape."

"Butch Devalon won the race today. Your feud with him has heated up over the last few weeks. Any comment?"

Dale smiled. "I don't have anything against Butch. I hope he does well. Of course I'd rather see him in my rearview than ahead of me, but I've got nothing against him. He knows that."

Dale put a hand on Tim's shoulder as they walked away. "You have a good day out here?"

"Yeah, it was good," Tim said. "Thanks for helping get me back here."

"Where'd you learn that trick with the hose and the funnel?"

"Just something I thought up on the spot."

"That pretty much saved my hide," Dale said. "I'd have come out of there like a piece of burnt toast if you hadn't fixed that thing up."

Tim nodded.

They walked to the hauler, and the whole #21 team came out to meet Dale, clapping and patting him on the back. Dale gave them an update on Jimmy's condition, then went inside to change out of his fire suit.

Tim waited with Kellen as the teams packed up—something he'd done a thousand times before. It was kind of nice not to have to do anything, not to get his hands dirty, but part of him wished he was still doing that because it would mean his dad would still be alive.

He wandered past the haulers and watched people at a fence overlooking the trucks. A woman with short hair looked straight at him. He did a double take. Could it be?

"Tim," Dale called, "you ready?"

Tim watched the woman turn and disappear. He wondered if the woman could really have been *her*.

Chapter 27
Big Day

TIM WOKE UP early on Thursday. There was no school because of some teacher study day, so he figured he'd sleep in. But the smells wafting down the stairs from the kitchen overwhelmed him and made his eyes open. He looked at the clock and rolled over, then stuffed a pillow over his head. The morning sun was bright through the slats of the window blinds.

When he couldn't stand it any longer, he got out of the covers and sat on the edge of the bed, looking at himself in the mirror. He needed a haircut. He needed some of that medicine Jamie used for her acne—though she had none compared to him. He needed to work out more. He looked skinny, even to himself.

He dressed and shoved a #14 hat over his bed hair. If he didn't take a shower, his hair stood up in the back and made him look like a walking chicken.

He was surprised to hear more voices than just Dale's and Mrs. Maxwell's in the kitchen. Jamie was saying something to Kellen when Tim turned the corner into the kitchen and almost took his head off on a streamer stretched across the doorway. Everybody stopped talking and looked at him like he was some kind of alien. Eggs were on a hot plate, sausage and bacon were sizzling in the pan, and there were pancakes and fresh syrup from one of the little stands alongside the road. Of course, Mrs. Maxwell also had a big bowl of fresh fruit on the table—bananas and strawberries and grapes and pineapple and even kiwis. That's what Jamie was munching on.

Tim looked around at the kitchen like it was some foreign country. Usually they didn't eat breakfast together because of their different schedules. Then he saw it. Above the light hanging over the middle of the table was a sign saying, Happy Birthday.

Dale started the song, and the others laughed at how off-key he was. When they got to "Happy birthday, dear Tim . . . ," Tim started laughing and shaking his head.

"What's the matter?" Dale said. "Think we'd forget?"

"It's not that I thought you'd forget," Tim said. "I didn't even remember."

"You forgot your own birthday?" Kellen said.

"We didn't make much of it when I was with my dad," Tim said. "We'd have dinner out, maybe, and he'd usually buy me something. . . ."

Tim's voice trailed off as he thought of his birthday a year ago. He'd gone to his father's funeral. Charlie Hale had delivered the rest of Tim's belongings from the hauler. Tyson and Vera picked him up afterward, apologizing for not making it to the service. Something about car problems and taking a wrong turn, but both of them were dressed for an all-day picnic, not a funeral. Then the long drive to the Slades' place.

"I made all your favorites," Mrs. Maxwell said, putting a plate at the end of the table. She poured him a glass of freshly squeezed orange juice and uncovered a dish of hash browns that were dark and crunchy the way Tim liked them. They were lightly salted and peppered and ready to douse with ketchup.

"Wow," Tim said. "I've never even seen a breakfast like this at a restaurant. I can't wait until dinner."

Kellen ran into the living room and came back with a package. "Can he open it now?"

"Let's let him eat first," Dale said. "We'll open presents later."

"Oh, come on, Dad," Kellen pleaded. "Just one?

Please?" He begged like a puppy that needed to go outside really bad.

"Go ahead, Dad," Jamie said. "It's just one present."

"You want to open one?" Dale said.

Tim shrugged. "There's more than one?"

Dale nodded to Kellen and he handed it to Tim. Tim opened it gingerly, but Kellen obviously couldn't stand that because he edged in, ripping the paper and throwing it around the room.

"Whoa," Tim said, pulling out a shiny jacket. On the back it said, Velocity High School.

"You've been here long enough to show some school spirit," Kellen said.

"Put it on," Jamie said.

"I don't want to get ketchup on it."

"Silly, you can take it off again before you eat."

"Okay." Tim put it on and everybody clapped. He bowed, trying to remember when he'd ever had this much attention.

Tim ate until he felt like his stomach would pop. Then Dale drove them to the local go-kart track. He paid for an all-day pass and even got in and raced Tim, Kellen, and Jamie. At lunchtime, Mrs. Maxwell brought subs, and Dale had to head over to Lowe's Motor Speedway with the crew.

"I'll see you tonight," Dale said.

Tim shook hands with him. “I really appreciate this. It’s . . . well, a lot more than I expected.”

Dale smiled. “You deserve a celebration. I’m glad you’re having a good time.”

Chapter 28
Gifts

JAMIE FELT comfortable around Tim, not as a boyfriend or romantic interest but as a younger brother who knew a lot about racing. After all, he was a year and a half younger than her—an eternity to people her age—and he wasn't as annoying as Kellen. She loved her younger brother and would defend him like a mother lion, but she also got tired of him at times.

Jamie wanted to give Tim something for his birthday but couldn't think of anything good. Her mom suggested she take him to the opening of a new action movie. It was a true guy flick with a few car chases and lots of explosions, but Jamie didn't mind those. She invited Cassie along too.

"Jamie's got a date!" Kellen said when he found out at dinner.

Jamie could have twisted the little runt's arm off right there, but she held her tongue. "Not a date, just a present. Cassie's springing for ice cream afterward."

Tim looked a little uneasy.

"You want to go, don't you?" she said.

"Yeah, sure. I've been wanting to see it."

He said it in a convincing way, but somehow Jamie picked up that he was a little nervous.

They ate dinner with the family, and Tim opened his other presents. One was a collectable die-cast car he'd mentioned to her dad, and another was an updated cell phone with the coolest design she'd ever seen. It was thinner than Tim's black comb he kept in his back pocket, and it looked like a car dashboard when it was opened.

Her mom handed Tim a heavy, book-shaped box. "This is from all of us."

Tim opened it and pulled out a devotional book for NASCAR fans with a bright cover. He flipped through it and thanked her, then picked up a new Bible, the same kind that Jamie used. Tim opened the front flap and read what her mom had inscribed there. "'To Tim, from the Maxwells, with all our love.'

"Thank you," Tim said. "I've never had a Bible of my own, except the old ratty one of my dad's. This is real nice." There was an uncomfortable silence, and Tim looked at each of them and fumbled with the Bible and the devotional, trying to get them back in the box. When he did, he shifted from one foot to the other in an awkward dance. Then he kind of smiled, though he tried hard not to show his front teeth for some reason.

"I don't think I've ever had a day like this one. I had a lot of fun with you guys. And I don't know why you all are so nice to me. I probably don't say thank you enough. But I appreciate it."

There were tears in her mom's eyes. She smoothed the tablecloth out, dabbed at an eye, and went over to Tim and hugged him. When she pulled back, her eyes were red. "Happy birthday, Timmy."

Kellen sighed. "I thought this was supposed to be a party, not a boo-hoo fest."

That made Tim laugh, and Dale came over and put an arm around him. "We're proud of you, Tim. Now you two better get going and pick up Cassie."

Jamie grabbed her keys and tried to wipe her eyes so no one would see her. "We'll be back a little late."

"Oh, Tim, I almost forgot," her mom said. "Some mail came for you today. I'll just put it on your bed, and you can see it when you get back."

Chapter 29
The Movie

TIM SAT UP front until they got to Cassie's house. It was a nice place with white shutters, a picket fence, and flowers growing out of every pot on the front porch. It looked like there were flowers growing everywhere.

"Cassie's parents will want to say hello," Jamie said. "Why don't you go in with me?"

"We gonna make the movie on time? I like to see the trailers."

"We're fine," Jamie said.

"Okay." Tim went to the porch, and the smell was like walking into one of those candle stores at the mall. It smelled so good that he wanted to bottle the aroma and sell it to little old ladies who loved flowers.

The Strowers were nice people with nice clothes and nice smiles. They even had a nice dog who didn't bark, and Tim wondered if it was a Christian dog. It just sat there looking at him with floppy ears and didn't move—except for his tail. Big eyes studying Tim like it knew he wasn't one of "them" and that he'd probably never crack open that Bible the Maxwells gave him except maybe to make people think he was reading it.

They chatted for a few minutes. Then Cassie said they should be going.

Tim opened the car door for her and Cassie said she'd sit in the back, but Tim beat her to the seat. When she got in, Cassie turned and handed him a card. He tried not to roll his eyes or anything, but he could guess what kind of card it would be. Probably a picture of Jesus on the front with his arms open, begging Tim to become a Christian. Or maybe a picture of an eagle that said, "Soar for the Lord!" Or a card that said a donation had been made in his name for some missionary in Tora Bora. Something like that.

He opened it and found a simple card that said "Happy Birthday" on a cake. Inside was a gift card to an online NASCAR store. Cassie had written a note on the blank space.

Tim,

I hope you have a great birthday. Enjoy your gift card. Thanks for being a friend. I love it when you talk in church.

Your friend, Cassie

Tim felt goose bumps down his back. No special verse for him. No prayer for his soul. Just a heartfelt message. Cassie was one of those sold-out Christians who Tim thought at first was only interested in getting him to come to church and be like them, but the more he hung around with her, the more it seemed like she really liked him. He could count on one hand the number of people who fell into that category, outside the Maxwells.

"Thanks," Tim said, slipping the gift card into his wallet. "This is great."

"Splurge on yourself," Cassie said. "Get those #14 woolly socks."

They were inside the #1 theater when Tim asked if either wanted popcorn or something to drink. He said he'd be right back.

I can't believe I'm sitting with two gorgeous girls, Tim thought. *Some birthday.*

He checked the board above the concessions stand and couldn't believe the prices. He and his dad hadn't gone to many movies, but when they did, his dad would never buy popcorn or candy because he said it was so expensive. Tim always thought his dad was just being cheap, but now he knew why the man carried Raisinets in his pocket into the theater. He couldn't go back empty-handed, though, or Jamie and Cassie would think *he* was cheap.

"Can I help you?" the girl behind the counter said.

Tim looked at the prices again. The difference between a small and a huge popcorn was only a couple of dollars, so he went ahead and bought a bucket and hoped Cassie and Jamie would share some. He got a few pushes of butter too, handed over his money, and jammed the change in his pocket.

As he turned to head back to the theater, he bumped into a black-jacketed guy with sunglasses and spilled most of his popcorn. Butter dripped on the guy's boots, which Tim guessed cost more than all the popcorn in the place.

"So you're clumsy *and* a cheater," Chad Devalon said. He hadn't seen how many butter spots were on his boots or his jeans that looked so tight Tim didn't know how the guy could breathe.

"Sorry. I didn't see you there," Tim said.

Chad finally noticed the butter on his pants and his boots and jumped back, cursing. He grabbed a few napkins from a dispenser and bent over, trying to wipe the spots away, but it didn't do any good.

"You are such a loser," Chad muttered, gritting his teeth. He stood up and slapped the popcorn tub out of Tim's hands, scattering the rest on the floor.

"What's wrong?" a girl said, coming from the bathroom area. She had a dark complexion, and Tim thought he recognized her but couldn't place her face.

"This loser ruined my new boots," Chad said. "Come on. Let's get out of here." He put his arm around the girl, then glanced back at Tim. "Take a good look at him, Rosa. That kid's going to jail. Just like his mommy."

Tim's heart raced. He wanted to run after Chad, jump on him from behind, and smash his face into the carpet. Instead, he watched them leave the theater and walk to the valet, who went for Chad's car. Then Tim bent over and scooped up the popcorn on the floor and tossed it in the trash.

The trailers were on when Tim got back to his seat, but he couldn't concentrate on them. Some Western with a megastar, a romantic comedy people laughed at, and a little girl with a magic dog.

Jamie leaned over to him. "What about the popcorn?"

Rosa's face and her voice kept going through Tim's mind. "Not hungry," he said.

Tim couldn't focus on the movie. Even the chase scenes couldn't take away the sting of Chad's words.

Afterward, they had ice cream at one of those fancy places where they put candy bars and peanuts in your ice cream and mix it together on a cutting board.

When they got home, he thanked Jamie.

"Did you like the movie?" she said.

"Yeah, it was good. A great ending to my day." Tim went to his room and flipped on the light. The Bible and the devotional book were there on top of his other gifts. Beside them were three pieces of mail. The top one was from Charlie Hale, the hauler driver he'd spent a lot of time with at the track. It was a goofy card supposed to make you laugh, but Tim didn't. Inside Charlie had written, "Happy 15th birthday, Tim." A $10 and a $5 bill fell onto the bed.

He's only a year off, Tim thought.

The second card had a return address from Florida. It had a race car on the front with a #16 on it. Inside was a note written in fancy handwriting, the kind Tim always wished he had but knew he never would. It was so curvy and curly he had to concentrate in order to read it.

Dear Tim,

I'm hoping the move to North Carolina has been a good one for you. I talked with Mrs. Maxwell the other day, and she told me how well you're doing in school, that you have a job with the team, and that you've become part of their family. I couldn't be happier for you.

I hope this is a great birthday and that one day my husband and I will get to come to a race where you're working or driving or whatever it is you would do.

God bless and happy birthday.

Lisa

Lisa was the social worker who had spent time with Tim and had arranged the move to the Maxwells'. She was one person who had made his stay in Florida better.

The last letter had no return address, but the postmark was from somewhere called Sylacauga, Alabama. He didn't know anybody from there and couldn't imagine who it would be from.

It was another card, one of those kinds that plays a song when you open the front flap. This one played a tune from a current superhero movie. He smiled, then looked at the bottom.

Timmy,

I saw you at the Talladega race. I'm so proud of you for going back there. That must have been hard. I hope your birthday was everything you wanted it to be.

I hope to see you soon.

Love,

Mom

Chapter 30
Considering Tim

THE NEXT THREE RACES didn't go quite as planned for Jamie's dad. Racing at Lowe's Motor Speedway was like playing a home game—the track wasn't that far away, so her dad didn't have to travel. He finished 15th there, a disappointing run after his success in the earlier Chase races. The only good news was that three of the Chase competitors had DNFs after their names, which killed them in the points standing.

At the half mile in Martinsville, a track her dad had found success on earlier in his career, he got bunched up late in the race with the middle of the pack and finished ninth. The only good thing about the race was that Butch Devalon got spun out with five laps to go and finished 16th. Jamie tried to hide her excitement at that because she knew there were always cameras around.

At Atlanta, the scene of one of her dad's worst crashes, he finished sixth, with a rookie driver who wasn't even in the Chase taking first place. Every time her dad raced here, Jamie flashed back to "the crash," as it had become known in the family. Jamie had been watching the race at home on TV with her mom. Kellen was just a little thing toddling around the house and looking for his favorite pacifier. On the frontstretch her dad was bumped and thrown into the rear of another car, turning sideways then, like some car-monster, rising into the air. His car had flipped—with two cars actually going underneath him while he was in the air—and skidded on its hood into the grassy infield. Her mom had quickly taken her out of the room, but that image stayed with her. Her dad had suffered a concussion, three broken ribs, and a dislocated shoulder, but he was back in the car the next week. Some called him crazy. Others called him tough. That crash was played and replayed on just about every NASCAR highlight reel Jamie had ever seen.

It all came down to the last three races. Her dad was in the fifth spot—Butch Devalon in second. Jamie thought the whole season would be worth it if he could just finish higher than Devalon.

As for Jamie's racing, she decided to concentrate on her dad's finish in the Chase and ramp up for next year in the East series. News had come of a 16-year-old who had just missed being the champion, and Jamie envied the kid. Because of finances and her schedule, she hadn't been able to race that series. Of course, being one of the top three in the experimental school and her qualifying her dad's car at Denver had helped give her a reputation. A few sponsors had contacted her dad about her, but no teams had offered her a spot. She kept in good shape, going to the gym almost every day. Between that, schoolwork, her part-time job delivering auto parts, and church, she didn't have much time to breathe.

The Tuesday before Texas, Tim came to Jamie right after she got home from the gym. It wasn't normal that he came up to her at all. Usually he stayed in the background doing whatever chore her dad gave him at the garage. He'd become a bit more outgoing since coming to live with them, but he was still shy and guarded around almost everyone. It surprised her to see him at her car when she got out. She wanted to go inside, take a shower, and head to the auto parts place. She was going to be late as it was.

"I got a favor to ask," Tim said.

"Sure. What is it?"

"Could I ride with you to your work?"

"I guess so. But I have to do some runs once I get there. How are you going to get back?"

"I can walk if I have to," Tim said. "Or I'll just meet you back there at closing."

"Okay, I can call your cell and tell you what time I'll be back."

On the way to the store, Jamie probed Tim, trying to find out what he was up to.

Tim stared at the road ahead with a half smile. "I think I figured something out."

"What?"

"I'll tell you if I'm right."

At the auto parts place, Jamie put her work shirt on over her T-shirt and buttoned it up. Tim walked through the parking lot and north toward a park. On the other side was downtown Velocity. She wondered why he was going that way. Something inside told her more was going on here than just a walk in the park.

Jamie had gone to Cassie's house to watch a movie last week, and the two had never even put the DVD in the player. They sat in the living room and talked about God and racing, boys (of course), and where they would be in five years. Or 10. Cassie said that in 10 years Jamie would have at least three championships under her belt. Jamie said Cassie would be known as "the diabetic evangelist to the Congo," something Cassie laughed at pretty hard.

Cassie was the one who brought up Tim. "I really

think it's great that your parents had a vision for taking him in. Where do you think he is spiritually?"

Jamie set the bowl of popcorn they were sharing on the coffee table. It was freshly popped, not the microwave kind. "He seems kind of like a leaf blown in the wind, you know? My dad has taken some of his talents and gifts and has really channeled him in a good direction, but it almost feels like we're just waiting for the other shoe to drop. That he's going to wind up in trouble or do something to make things harder for himself."

Cassie took a drink of soda. "Like he's going to sabotage what he has because he doesn't deserve the breaks he's been given?"

"Exactly. My mom says that sometimes people get so many bad breaks that they start thinking that's what they're supposed to get. And when things go the other way, they don't think they deserve it."

Cassie sighed. "What happened to Tim's mom?"

Jamie shook her head. "We don't know. My dad tried to find out through the jerk of a guy Tim was staying with down in Florida. I don't know why Tim's dad would ever give him control over his estate."

"What did he say?" Cassie said.

"He hadn't heard from Tim's mom in years. But the social worker in Florida called my mom about something strange."

Cassie sat forward. "What?"

"A woman somehow found out that she was Tim's social worker. She asked a lot of questions about Tim, almost like she knew him."

"She thinks it might be Tim's mom?"

Jamie shrugged. "I guess it could be. She was awfully interested in Tim. The social worker saw the article about our family and said to watch out for anybody trying to contact him."

"I guess there are some crazy people out there."

Jamie grew silent, thinking about Tim's life. "Sometimes I look at him and wonder what's going on inside. He acts like nothing bothers him. Like there's nothing going on at all. But you know he has to be thinking stuff."

Cassie nodded. "Still waters run deep."

"What's that mean?"

"Just that Tim's a deep pool. There's more going on inside than it appears."

"Yeah, I see. The other day he asked to see my cell phone. I think he was setting something up on his new one, but he wouldn't tell me anything. I finally gave it to him. I really think he needs a friend his age to talk with."

"What he needs most of all is to know how much God loves him. There are times when I'll see him in church, and he looks like a lost puppy waiting for somebody to pick him up. I prayed that a strong, Christian man would come into his life, but then I realized that prayer had already been answered."

"What do you mean?"

"Your dad," Cassie said. "Don't you see how perfectly everything fit together? God worked that whole thing out so Tim could come here and be part of your family. Who knows what he has in store for him in the future."

"Wait. I don't understand everything about how God works yet, but you think God killed Tim's dad so Tim would come here? From what I hear, Tim's dad was a Christian too."

"I'm not saying God caused the accident. I don't know how it all works either, but I do know he's in control. And it's no accident that Tim is here with you guys."

Jamie locked her car and moved to the front door of the auto parts place. She watched Tim disappear on the other side of the park as she walked inside to pick up her delivery list. Something didn't feel right, but she had to go to work.

[illegible]

[illegible]

[illegible]

[illegible]

[illegible]

Chapter 31
Recording

TIM OPENED his cell phone and scrolled through the different numbers he'd programmed. He'd been preparing for this for a few days. He dialed the Pit Stop and talked with Mrs. Flattery, who confirmed that Chad Devalon was there and was alone. Tim quickly dialed the cell number.

Chad answered with a "Yeah?"

"Meet me out here by your car," Tim said.

"Who is this?"

"Time we cleared this whole thing up," Tim said. "You'd better hurry before something happens." He hung up and walked through the shadows of the trees by the restaurant.

Chad ran out of the restaurant, turned the corner, and saw his car. The red Corvette was parked at the end—Tim guessed he parked so far away because he didn't want anyone to open a door and ding it. Chad looked relieved and slowed when he saw it.

"Nice car," Tim said, stepping out of the shadows.

Chad sneered. "What do *you* want?" He said *you* like Tim was a dung beetle.

Tim crossed his arms and leaned against a Dumpster. "I got to thinking about my hat and that race at Hickory, wondering who might have taken it. And when it showed up at your dad's garage, it was a bit strange."

Chad narrowed his eyes and shook his head. "I'm not talking to you, you loser. Just stay away from me." He turned and pushed the keyless entry that unlocked the car and opened the door.

"That's fine. When the cops find out what I know, they'll probably want to speak with you."

Chad turned. "What are you talking about?"

"I called Rosa. She told me the whole thing."

He shut the door. "What?"

"She told me she was the one who called me. Apologized, actually, which I thought was kind of nice seeing that she really does like you."

Chad stared at Tim. He reminded Tim of Jeff back in Florida. Shorter, stockier, but with all the attitude and swagger. "You expect me to believe a lie like that? Is that the best you can do?"

"I tried calling Kenny. I figured he was the one who took my hat and got it to you. And that you were the one who set fire to your dad's garage and planted my hat there. You rooked Rosa into helping you, knowing that she'd probably do what you told her to."

"You think I set the fire? How do you figure that?"

"Your dad gave Jamie a shot at you. He holds the purse strings. No wonder you're ticked off at him. This was a way to get back at him *and* make my life and the Maxwells' a bit more miserable."

"You're crazy," Chad said.

"It also makes sense that you would start a teeny little fire, because you wanted to hurt your dad, but not too much. Especially if he allows you a place on his team someday. Didn't figure on the gas can blowing, but you can't have everything."

Chad's face turned red. "You're just jealous because you don't even have a dad. And the one you did have was worthless. Everybody knows that."

Tim had been prepared for two reactions. Either Chad would get in his car and drive away or he'd lash out and fight. While he didn't like what he said about Tim's dad, Tim was encouraged by it. It meant he was on to something.

"The police know it wasn't me. They've seen the video of me outside when the fire starts. It was smart to get me there and tamper with the surveillance video, but it didn't make much sense to leave the other camera. Plus, you had a key to the garage, didn't you?"

Chad took a step toward him. "You don't know who you're dealing with, do you?"

"I got a pretty good idea. Just another scared and mixed-up kid like I am. You've got a lot more money and toys—" he pointed to the car—"but inside we're the same. Except I'm not the one who started that fire."

Chad was close enough to take a swing at Tim. He clenched his teeth. "You had the perfect motive for starting that fire. You watched the DVD of your dad getting smashed, and you saw it was my dad who started that accident."

Tim stared at him.

"Why didn't you tell anybody about that DVD?" Chad said, a smile crossing his lips. "I thought you'd go squealing to Maxwell or somebody at NASCAR. Crying for justice. Wanting to avenge your father's death. That's the perfect motive for starting the fire. Except you stayed quiet."

"I didn't start the fire," Tim said.

Chad shrugged. "Everybody thinks you did. The police can't prove it, but at least it's a distraction for Maxwell. My old man will never find out. The police have pretty much dropped it. They think it was vandals. And the only one who figured it out was a kid who used to live out of a hauler." He shook his head. "Life sure does strange things, don't it?"

"Yeah," Tim said. "But it's good to keep some of those strange things around just so you can remember them." He pulled out a minirecorder he had in his shirt pocket and clicked it off. "I figure this will clear things up pretty well for anybody who wants to know."

A look came over Chad's face. It was a mix of surprise and horror and disbelief. It was the exact look Tim had been hoping for. The one he'd dreamed about. Chad lunged for the recorder, and Tim saw why he was such a good driver. He had quick reactions. But because Tim had planned all of this, he was ready. He dodged Chad's grab and took off through the parking lot. He heard Chad behind him, his expensive sneakers pounding the pavement and getting closer.

Tim didn't have time to look both ways and ran into the street. Tires screeched, and he looked right as a red SUV locked its tires and came at him. Tim put up a hand to block it and turned his head, thinking he would be flying through the air like Superman at any second. But he didn't.

The smells of locked brakes and fresh rubber were

strong. A man got out and ran to the front of the SUV. "Are you okay? You just flew out in the middle of the street."

"I'm all right," Tim said, his heart pounding. He looked back at Chad and slipped the recorder into his breast pocket. "I should have been more careful."

"I don't know how I stopped," the man said. "You should be dead right now. There must be some angels up there watching out for you."

"Yeah," Tim said. "Probably an angel somewhere."

He crossed to the other side of the street and watched Chad return to the parking lot. When the Corvette fired up, Tim ran for another alley, pulled out his cell phone, and dialed Jamie. "Any chance you can pick me up?"

"I'm on a run right now, but I can be back that way in about 20 minutes," she said.

"No, that's okay. I'll just meet you at the parts store at closing."

Chapter 32
Confrontation

TIM WAS HIDING in the bushes when Jamie returned to the auto parts store. She asked him what he was doing back there, but he didn't answer. He just hopped in Maxie and closed the door. She clocked out and drove home with Tim remaining quiet.

"So, did you find out what you were hoping to find out?" she said.

He glanced at her. "I've been trying to get ahold of your dad. You know where he is?"

She shook her head. "He's either at the garage or at home. You didn't have to work today?"

Tim was already dialing the garage. He hit the right front fender of his phone. "Nobody there."

"What's up with you?" Jamie said. "You're acting funny."

Tim looked back at a car following

close behind them. "Take a right here. See if that car's following you."

Jamie pulled to the side of the road, and a newer Mustang passed. "Tim, stop acting so weird and tell me what's going on."

"I just need to get home so I can talk with your parents," Tim said. "Please." He said it with an urgency she'd never seen or heard from him.

"Okay, okay, sure."

They pulled into the driveway, and Tim was out before the car even stopped. She rolled her eyes. "Boys."

Her mom was in the kitchen listening to Tim. Jamie went upstairs to change and heard her mom call her dad from the front porch.

"What's up?" Kellen said, coming out of his room.

"Something to do with Tim," Jamie said. "And I don't think it's good."

Kellen ran downstairs so fast it sounded like pistons firing in an engine.

Jamie followed as soon as she heard a car pull up in the driveway, scattering gravel all over the lawn. Two doors opened and closed and there was shouting.

Jamie rushed through the front door and saw Chad Devalon pointing a finger at Tim and yelling, "Give it back!"

"Tell him to hand it over, Maxwell," Butch Devalon said. "This has gone far enough."

Chad rushed at Tim and it looked like he was going to hit him, but her dad stepped in front of him and cut him off.

"Tell him to give back my recorder," Chad said, his face twisted. He looked like was going to cry.

Tim stood there with his hands in his back pockets, edging away from the confrontation.

Butch Devalon came up behind his son and tried to move around Jamie's dad.

"Tim, go inside the house until we can sort this out," her dad said. He turned and whispered something to him.

Tim ran up the stairs and into the house, passing Jamie without a word or a look.

Jamie moved down a step and stood beside her mom. "What in the world is going on?" she whispered.

"Chad says Tim stole a microrecorder from him. Tim says it's his."

"Now let's settle down and figure out what this is about," her dad said.

"That kid got into Chad's car and stole his recorder," Butch Devalon said. "The little pyromaniac is a thief too. I can't believe a Christian man like you would tolerate such behavior."

"Well, we haven't figured out what kind of behavior he's having," her dad said. "Chad, how long have you had this recorder?"

"I don't know. A couple of weeks, maybe."

"Where did you buy it?"

"At . . . an electronics store. Best Buy or Circuit City. I can't remember which."

"You keep the receipt?" her dad said.

"Of course not. Why would I want to keep the receipt?"

"Tim says he bought that recorder with his own money. He's in getting the receipt right now."

"That is such a crock!" Chad yelled. "I don't care what he has in there. It's mine. Dad, he's going to hide it. I told you this would happen!"

"Are you sure you're not just upset about what's on the recorder?" her dad said.

"No, I just want it back," Chad said, but his face showed something more.

"Maxwell, if you don't bring that recorder out here right now, I'm going to go in and get it myself."

Her dad straightened. "No, you're not going in my house." He looked at Jamie. "Go get Tim."

She walked inside and ran down the stairs, only to find Tim's room empty. She found him in the kitchen, uploading the contents of the recorder onto the computer. "Is that really yours?"

"Yeah, I got it with my birthday money."

"Dad wants you outside."

"Yeah, almost done." He kept looking at the screen, then ejected the recorder. He clicked the Play button on the computer, and Jamie heard Chad's voice. "You had the perfect motive for starting that fire. You watched the DVD of your dad getting smashed, and—"

Tim stopped the recording and hurried outside, pulling out his wallet and holding out the receipt to her mom.

"This is legit, Butch," her mom said. "This is his machine. He bought it with—"

"It's mine!" Chad shouted, pushing past his dad and running toward Tim like some kindergartner who'd had his favorite blanket stolen.

Jamie moved in front of Tim.

Chad stopped, his mouth twitching. "Move out of the way, Jamie. I don't want to hurt you, but I swear . . ."

"Give it to him, Tim," her dad said.

"Dad!" Jamie said.

"Dad!" Kellen said.

"Dale!" her mom said.

Tim just stood there.

"Go ahead," her dad said. "Toss it to him."

"Dad, I heard what he said to Tim," Jamie said. "He was cruel. Something about him—"

"Jamie," her dad said, and she knew he meant for her to be quiet.

Tim looked at her dad like he was about to cut Tim's heart out, like he was saying, *Don't you believe me?*

"Toss it to him, Tim," her dad said.

Tim tossed the recorder and Chad caught it in one hand. He looked at the display, then hit a button and it beeped. Chad's face showed relief. He tossed the recorder back to Tim, turned, and walked to the car.

Butch Devalon looked like he had just found out he was in the wrong line at the Department of Motor Vehicles. He stared at Chad walking away, then at Tim, then at her dad.

"There's something you should know, Mr. Devalon," Tim said. "It's about the fire at your garage."

"Dad, come on!" Chad hollered from the car.

"I know who started the fire," Tim said.

Devalon narrowed his eyes at Tim. "You ready to confess?"

Jamie's dad went over and put a hand on Tim's shoulder. "Tim didn't do it. It was somebody a lot closer to home." Her dad nodded at the car as it fired up and Chad honked the horn.

"You don't have any proof of that," Devalon said.

"I had it on this recorder," Tim said. "That was why he was so upset about it."

It looked like the wheels in Butch Devalon's mind were turning. He opened his mouth, but the horn honked again. He looked at Tim. "Stay away from my boy—you hear me?" He walked across the lawn and drove away.

Chapter 33
Running in Circles

TIM LET THE MAXWELLS HEAR the recording.

Dale's face was pained, as if listening was the hardest thing he'd ever done. When it was over, he turned to Tim. "What DVD was Chad talking about?"

Tim told them, then retrieved it from his room and played it for them. Mrs. Maxwell couldn't watch—she went into the kitchen. Jamie turned away when the accident happened. Dale and Kellen watched the whole thing.

When the video went into slow motion, Dale let out a grunt and ran a hand through his hair. "Why didn't you tell us about this?"

"I didn't know who it was from," Tim said. "And I didn't know what I was going to do about it."

"How'd you fit the pieces together?" Mrs. Maxwell said.

"The hat had a lot to do with it. I wasn't 100 percent sure when I decided to go after Chad, but I thought I could get him to give it up if he was guilty."

"That part about Rosa," Jamie said. "Did you really talk to her?"

"No. But when I went back over the call, I thought something in the woman's voice sounded familiar. If Chad had called her when we were talking in the parking lot, he probably wouldn't have spilled the beans."

Dale shook his head. "I know you were just trying to get information, but lying to Chad was not the answer. You know that, right?"

Tim put his head down. "Yes, sir."

There were more questions, but Tim finally went to his room.

A few minutes later Dale and Mrs. Maxwell came in.

"I'm really sorry this happened," Dale said. "Part of the reason to bring you up here was to protect you from stuff like this."

"What about Chad?" Tim said. "Should we talk to the police?"

Dale folded his arms. "I can talk with the officer who was here. We've become pretty good friends. My guess is that Butch wouldn't press charges against his own son."

"Why wouldn't he listen?" Tim said. "Why wouldn't he want to know the truth? He has to know his son lies."

Mrs. Maxwell was sitting on the floor and she leaned forward. "Tim, it's part of our nature not to want to know the truth. We like to hide. From ourselves. From God. We fool ourselves into thinking things that aren't true. Butch has always believed that if he's successful on the track and wins a lot of races and makes money, he'll be happy. And his family too. But Chad has been crying out for a real father since he was little."

"My hope is that all of this will help them both," Dale said. "It could be a wake-up call for Butch to change his input into Chad's life. But it probably won't."

Tim thought about what the two were saying. They probably thought he was the same as Butch, running from God, not wanting to think about the truth. He'd actually read a few of the devotionals, and it was the one about the spotter that got to him. The spotter in a race sees all the cars and the whole racetrack while the driver can see only a little way in front, to the sides, and behind. His vision is limited.

The book said that God is like that spotter. He knows everything, sees everything, and knows the beginning from the end. He knows what's coming up ahead, what's gone on behind, and the very best route to take.

At the end of the devotional, the writer gave a couple of verses from the Bible. Proverbs 3:5-6. Tim didn't know what that said or even where Proverbs was, but he opened to the front and found what page Proverbs 3 was located on and flipped through until he found it.

Trust in the Lord with all your heart;
do not depend on your own understanding.
Seek his will in all you do,
and he will show you which path to take.

Tim had read the verses again. His problem wasn't believing that God was there. Tim knew deep down that he was. His problem was that he didn't trust him. After what happened with his dad, he couldn't imagine putting his life in the hands of someone who was so mean as to let his own father be taken.

"So you think we should let all of this go?" Tim said. "Just forget about it?"

Dale pursed his lips. "I'm going to ask God for wisdom. I don't know the exact thing to do, but maybe God can even use something like this to bring somebody to him. I don't think it's right just to look the other way, but all of us need grace."

"What do you mean?"

"Forgiveness when we don't deserve it. It's what God offers us."

Mrs. Maxwell turned to him. "But one of the conditions God puts on it is our recognizing we need that forgiveness. We have to confess the wrong we've done, own up to it."

"True," Dale said. "Until Chad and Butch come to that point, they're just running in circles."

After they left, Tim held the DVD of his father's accident in his hands and sat back on his bed. He finally knew the truth about who had given it to him. He also knew the truth about who had caused the accident. But what about himself? He'd done a lot of bad things in his life. Some of them he'd made right—like the money he stole from that old woman Mrs. Rubiquoy in Florida. He'd taken it back to her, and she told him something he'd never heard before. That God had something special for him. That he wanted to work through someone like Tim.

"I'm not sure I even believe in God," Tim had said.

"Well, that's okay," Mrs. Rubiquoy had said. "He believes in you."

The woman had told him not to forget that she was waiting to hear that he'd found the Lord. Tim smiled at the memory of her wrinkled face and picked up his Bible. He stared at it a long time, then put it on his nightstand, turned off the light, and went to sleep.

Chapter 34
On the Radio

IT WAS WEIRD for Jamie to be in Texas with her dad having a shot at the championship. Usually when they were here he was playing the part of the spoiler, trying to race ahead of the big boys and steal a win while they were battling it out for the championship. Now he was on the other side of things, looking at the rest of the field from the front rather than the back.

However, the last three races were going to be long and nothing was going to be easy. That became evident when her dad had trouble with the car before the race and had to qualify the backup without much practice time.

There were so many requests by the media for interviews that Chloe Snowe was running frantically and burning up her cell phone. She put a list of interviews in front of Jamie's dad—

everything from the major NASCAR magazines to a Christian radio station in town that wanted him to come to the studio for their morning program.

"I'll definitely do that one," her dad said, pointing to the Christian station.

"But there are a lot bigger stations—"

"I want to do that one," he said. "I talk about racing all the time, but I hardly ever get to talk about my faith with any kind of depth. I want to do that one, and if any of the magazines want to come along, we'd be glad to have them."

/////

Jamie's concept of a Christian radio station was an old building with dusty, fake plants in the corner and old equipment other stations threw out. She was surprised when she and her dad walked into a new office building and were ushered to an elevator and to the top of the building with a view of the Metroplex that was second to none.

They had listened to the station on the way, and Jamie tried to imagine the people behind the voices. They were nothing like she pictured them. She figured the main host, a guy with a voice deeper than the Grand Canyon, would be big and burly like a bear. Instead, he was shorter than her and skinnier than Tim. There were traffic and news reporters, both women, who were pretty and welcomed them. Jamie thought they'd all have bloodshot eyes and bed hair, but they didn't.

Jamie sat in the control room and watched her dad through the huge window. He autographed a couple of shirts for listeners and had a few pictures taken while music played.

When it was over, the host pulled the silver microphone to him and put on his headphones. "Dale, anybody who knows NASCAR knows about your stand for God, your integrity, the way you handle yourself out there. And I think God has really honored you by putting you in this position of racing for the cup."

"Well, I don't look at it as God honoring *me* as much as it is him working out his plan in my life," her dad said. "I don't see myself any more in his plan now than I did earlier this year when I was in trouble with a sponsor who thought I might not be a good investment. God takes us through the ups and downs and teaches us through the hard times. I'd much rather be in first than 43rd place, of course, but I'll admit he's taught me a lot through the spinouts and crashes."

The traffic reporter leaned forward. "Your daughter is with you this morning, and I know she has a promising career ahead of her. What's it like for a dad to watch his daughter do something so dangerous?"

"Well, you mentioned a couple of accidents in your last report. It's dangerous just driving to work. I've always wanted my kids to follow Jesus, and whatever he gives them to do is okay with me. I want my daughter to have a chance to do what she wants, and if that's racing, then I'm fine with it."

"Does your wife feel the same way?" the news reporter said with a chuckle.

"She's had her moments," her dad said. "But you have to remember, because of my schedule, she's the one who's been driving Jamie to most of her races in the past few years."

The engineer in the room started a music bed underneath them, and the host took control. "One more question, Dale. If you don't win the championship, will this season still be a success?"

"I guess that depends on how you define success. If winning is the only measure of that, then there are a lot of drivers and teams that will be disappointed. But if your definition is doing what God has called you to, doing your best and touching as many people with God's love as possible, then that changes everything."

"You still want to win though, right?" the host said.

Her dad laughed. "I didn't come down here to lose."

Chapter 35
The Call

TIM WALKED past the garage to the pits, rubbing his hands together, hoping he wouldn't run into any of the Devalons, and checking the leader board. Dale had started a dismal 35th, and the car was terribly loose until the first pit stop. Tim knew it was a continual adjustment process to bring a backup car up to speed. The only question was whether they had enough race to get him to the front.

It was a 500-mile race, but it wasn't until lap 295 that Dale made his way to the front and was able to stay out of a pit stop and actually lead a lap, giving him those extra points. When the leaders came out, Dale was pushed back to 16th place with a car that desperately needed fuel and new tires.

"We need to come in for a final push, Dale," T.J. said. "Your right side is really getting thin."

"Just hoping for a yellow," Dale said.

On the next lap, the team got what it wanted, though it was at the expense of a friend. The #47 car spun in turn four, then came back down the track, causing the car in third place to clip the second-place car. Dale pitted under the yellow and picked up several spots. There were 15 cars on the lead lap.

"I hate like the dickens that those guys are out," Dale said. "Are they both at the garage?"

"Yeah, there's a lot of damage to both cars," T.J. said. "I doubt either one will make it back."

Dale had moved into the top 10, chasing Butch Devalon and several others by the end of the race. After some lead changes at the end, the #11 car took the lead and held off the field for the win, putting him in first place in the Chase. Dale finished eighth—a great race for having to use the backup car.

"After starting a lot lower than we wanted, we're happy with that finish," Dale said to an on-track reporter after the race. "We kept making adjustments and doing what we had to do."

"You're sitting right now at fourth place, 10 points back of the leader, but with three other drivers to jump over by the end," the reporter said. "Can you do it?"

Dale chuckled. "I guess we're going to find out, aren't we?"

In the hauler, the whole crew met, and it made

Tim feel like old times with a team. Usually he had to pack up and tear down for the end of the race so they could get on the road, but a few times when the team had done well, Tim joined his dad and the others for a debriefing about the race.

"We couldn't have done this without you guys in the pits today," Dale said. "I felt like every time we came in, you were as fast if not faster than any team out there. That builds a lot of confidence and makes me excited to come in rather than dreading it."

"Scotty kept us out of a couple of wrecks," T.J. said. "And Dale's been driving like he was 20 years old."

"Don't forget the contraption Tim made at Talladega," Chloe said.

Everybody clapped, and Tim thought his head would explode with pride. Someone mentioned Jamie's feat at Denver that put them in position to even get in the Chase.

That's when Tim's cell phone rang. He moved out of the hauler so he wouldn't disturb the team and looked at the display. He didn't recognize the number. He answered and waited a minute because there was noise on the line.

"Timmy?" a woman said.

"Yeah, this is Tim."

The woman gasped. "It's Alex. I'm here in Dallas. I want to see you."

"Alex? How do I know you?"

"Alexandra," she said. "Your mom. I'm sorry I've been such a ghost. If you don't want to see me, I'll understand."

"Wait," Tim said, remembering Chad's trick. "Tell me something about you nobody else would know. Or something about Dad."

"What for?"

"I just need you to tell me something."

"Okay," she said tentatively. "Let's see. Your dad had a scar on his left shoulder. Do you remember that?"

"He said he got it from an alligator in the Everglades."

She laughed. "He got it crawling through the attic of the first house we rented. There were squirrels up there, and he was trying to flush them out. Cut it on an old, rusty nail."

"Really?" Tim said.

"He was a good man. I'm sure you know that."

"Yeah."

"Are you still at the track?" she said.

"They're getting ready to pack up. The Maxwells are staying one more night, and we'll get a flight out in the morning."

"Let me come see you," she said. "Where's your hotel?"

Tim told her and she asked him to repeat it so she could write it down. In the background was the clink of plates, the hum of voices, and music that sounded like some honky-tonk.

"I'll call you from the lobby. I'll let your cell ring once and you come down. Oh, and Timmy?"

"Yeah?"

"Don't tell the Maxwells, okay?"

"Why not?"

"Well, they might not understand, you know? Let's just keep this between you and me for now."

Tim was a nervous ball of energy at the hotel. The family had a late dinner and went to the Maxwells' room to watch TV coverage of the race and the interviews replayed. Tim put his cell phone on vibrate and kept his hand in a pocket, holding it and hoping it would ring soon.

He and Kellen went to their room and flipped on the TV, but Tim just stared out the window. Mrs. Maxwell called and said it was time to get some sleep, so they turned off the TV and Kellen was out like a light. He was a mouth breather and slurped and gurgled most of the night.

Tim lay there looking at the electric clock numbers that clicked by as fast as cold molasses. He put his pillows (the bed had about a dozen) up in a pile and tried to stay awake, but the lull of Kellen's breathing and the fatigue of the day caught up with him.

He closed his eyes for a minute and dreamed that his dad had come to Texas and his mom was riding with him in his truck, her arm around him. They were laughing and talking and having a good time. They couldn't see it, but Butch Devalon came up to a street beside them and T-boned their truck.

Tim woke up to find his cell vibrating. He jumped out of bed, still fully clothed, and ran to the elevator, not remembering he'd forgotten his key card on the nightstand until he punched the down button on the elevator. He got off at the lobby and tried to straighten his hair. In the elevator he had seen that he had the fuzzy chicken look.

The hotel was a fancy place with all the help dressed in uniforms or suits. Tim walked to the front lobby, where there were a few couches and chairs that looked so comfortable he thought he could sleep here if there wasn't so much noise of the door opening and closing with people coming in and out all night.

He spotted a blonde woman on one of the couches with a phone to her ear. It wasn't what he pictured his mom looking like, but he approached the couch and stopped to listen.

"I know," the woman said with a Southern twang.

"I told Donna the other day that I didn't want to hear any more excuses, but they keep coming."

The woman had a nice dress on and a ring that would choke a Clydesdale. Not exactly what he thought his mom would be wearing.

"Excuse me," someone said behind him.

Tim turned and immediately knew the woman was his mother. She had short, curly hair, and a vague image flashed through his mind from a picture he had kept. She had a pleasant face, with not too much makeup but enough to obscure some freckles. She seemed a little self-conscious about the space between her front teeth, because she didn't smile too wide when she saw Tim. Her eyes looked tired, like they'd been open way too long and had seen way too much, and there were lines at the corners, like a road map crossing the sides of her face.

She wore a buttoned shirt over a T-shirt and jeans that were torn on the leg. There were lots of kids who wore those kinds of jeans at his school, but they did it as a fashion statement. Tim had a feeling these were the only jeans she had.

They moved to a stone fireplace, out of earshot of anyone else.

"You're so tall," she said. "It's hard to think of you any bigger than when I last saw you. You had your little blanket and your favorite bear. What did your dad do with those?"

"He probably threw them out," Tim said. "I wore that cover out, and the bear fell apart."

"And your voice is so deep." She looked him over and smiled, keeping her lips together. "I can't believe I'm actually seeing you again and that you're not running away."

"Why would I do that?"

"Just because it's been so long and you're probably mad that I never came back. I wouldn't blame you for being angry."

"I'm not angry."

"You sure?" she said.

"Yeah. I mean, you're my mom." Tim studied the carpet. It had huge swirling designs in it. Interesting, for carpet. "I still have questions, you know. Like where you went and what you did and why it took so long to come see me. And why Dad would have Tyson and Vera take care of me, which they didn't."

"I'm the one to blame about that," she said. "We didn't have a ton of people to choose from, but I thought if anything happened to your dad, the closest place to me would be in Florida, and they were the only relatives down there."

"You knew you were going to Florida when you left?" Tim said.

"That was my plan. I wound up staying there longer than I wanted in a place I didn't want to be. But that's another story."

Tim looked at the carpet again, then back at his mom. He wasn't going to squander a chance to find out everything he could. After all, he had no idea if his mom would take off after this meeting and he'd never see her again. "Why did you get sent to prison?" Then, when he saw her face, he said, "I'm sorry. I shouldn't have asked that."

"No, it's okay. I was wondering how to tell you anyway. How'd you find out?"

Tim told her.

"It's a long story. The truth is, I got hooked up with a group of people who weren't good for me. I had a job as a chauffeur, driving people around and getting big tips. But I got into some financial trouble, and a friend offered to bail me out if I'd help him, just once. I agreed and I got caught." She held up both hands. "No excuses. I knew better and I let it happen."

"And you went to jail and did your time."

"Absolutely."

"Then why did you skip your parole? You were supposed to meet with an officer once a week, weren't you?"

She rubbed her hands together like there was something wrong with them, worried, looking around. Was she searching for an exit in case some police officers tracked her down? "Look. I'm not perfect. I've made a lot of mistakes. But I'm here to ask you something important. That's why I came."

"How did you get my phone number?" Tim said.

"Tyson gave me the number of that social worker, but she wasn't much help. After I saw the magazine article, I spoke with Charlie Hale. He got your number from Maxwell. He didn't know he was giving your number to Charlie to give to me, of course. That's how I got your address too."

"What do you want to ask me?"

His mom looked scared, and it was a weird feeling for Tim to watch someone older go through what he experienced in class every time he had to give a speech. "I was wondering . . ."

"Tim?" someone said behind him. He turned to see Mrs. Maxwell. She had puffy eyes, like she'd been asleep, and wore her bathrobe. "Is something wrong?"

"No," Tim said. "I just . . ." He looked back at his mother, then got tongue-tied. He checked the clock. It was one thirty in the morning.

"Kellen called our room and said you weren't in your bed. Dale was sound asleep, so I came here." She looked at Tim's mom. "Do I know you?"

"Not exactly, ma'am," his mom said, extending a hand. "Alexandra Carhardt."

The look on Mrs. Maxwell's face was priceless. If she'd have gotten the crown jewels of England as a birthday present, her expression wouldn't have been any more surprised. "Tim's mom? I'm so glad to meet you. Oh, you two have a lot of catching up to do. I'll leave you alone."

"No, it's okay," Tim's mother said. "I'm sorry I came so late. I just wanted to know if Tim would like to come live with me."

Chapter 36
Letting Go

JAMIE DIDN'T GET TO SEE Tim's mom because she left shortly after seeing him at the hotel. On the plane ride back to North Carolina the next morning the family was tight-lipped about the visit. Kellen and her dad played a racing video game together while Tim read. Jamie tried to talk with her mom about the situation, but her mom was clearly upset.

When they arrived at home, Jamie cornered her in her bedroom and closed the door. "What's going on, Mom?"

"Tim's mom wants him to come live with her. I think Tim is seriously considering it."

"Why shouldn't he?" Jamie said. "If I were living with some other family and you came back, I'd go with you."

"You know that's not the point," her mom said. "This woman has been out of Tim's life since he was little. Where's she been? Why did she abandon him? And why should we believe she's fit to be his mother now?"

Jamie shrugged. "I don't think that makes a difference to Tim. He looks excited to have his mom back."

"He's just getting a little stability in his life," her mom said in a huff. "I saw him reading that devotional we gave him. With all he's been through, the last thing he needs is a flighty mother to take him away."

Jamie sat on the bed and lay back on the lacy pillows arranged at the head. How many times had she and her mom talked about things like this? Only they were usually about Jamie—what choices to make, what path to take. She felt like somehow the tables were turning, like she was the one to help her mom see something instead of the other way around. She sat up and said, "How much of this is about what's best for Tim and how much is about you? What *you* want?"

Her mom stopped putting away her clothes and turned. Her face looked pained. "That's a fair question, and I'll admit I've grown accustomed to Tim. I think we've been good for him, and he's also been good for us. He fits here. It's not a perfect arrangement, but it's better than any of his other choices. I just don't want to see him get hurt again."

Jamie nodded. "I agree. But if there's one thing I've learned from you over the years, it's that if God really is in control, we can trust him to work things out."

"You observed that?"

Jamie smiled. "I think you need to give Tim the same amount of rope you gave me. Love him enough to let him go. Let him make a choice."

Her mom shook her head. "You know what he'll do."

"But are you going to tie him up and make him stay here or trust that God is working on him?"

Her mom leaned against her dresser, balling some clean laundry in her hands. "I want to fight for him. Nobody's ever fought for him." Tears came to her eyes. "When I think of how lonely he's been, how alone in so many things . . ."

Jamie hugged her mom, and tears came to her own eyes. "I know. I'm not saying it's going to be easy to let go. And I agree with you that he'd be better off here. But this has to be his choice."

Jamie nodded. "I agree. But there's one thing I've learned from you over the years. It's that if God really is in control, we can trust him to work things out."

"You're right [illegible]."

Jamie smiled. "I think you need to give Ian the same amount of rope you gave me. Love him enough to let him go. Let him make a choice."

Her mom shook her head. "You know what he'll do."

"But are you going to tie him up and make him stay here or trust that God is working in him?"

Her mom leaned against her dresser, holding some clean laundry in her hands. "I want to fight for him. Nobody's ever fought for him." Tears came to her eyes. "When I think of how lonely he's been, how [illegible] so many things . . ."

Jamie hugged her mom, and tears came to her own eyes. "There—I'm not saying it's going to be easy to let go. And chances with him [illegible] perfect. [illegible] But this has to be his choice."

Chapter 37
Phoenix

BEFORE TIM'S MOM LEFT the hotel, she had told him she'd call during the week. Tim checked his phone after each class and during lunch, but there were no messages. She hadn't said where she was living, and he hadn't pressed her about her troubles with the Florida authorities.

Even though Tuesday was his first day back (he had taken Monday off to return from the race), the week dragged by. Tim watched the coverage of the upcoming Phoenix race and listened to talk radio programs about who would be the winner. Everybody spoke of Dale Maxwell with respect, but nobody gave him a chance. The other teams had multiple drivers in the Chase, and Dale had such a small budget. It was David vs. Goliath, a bicycle against a souped-up motorcycle. Somehow Tim didn't think that bothered Dale. It probably helped him.

Mrs. Maxwell acted strange around Tim most of the week, putting on a pleasant face. He passed her computer and saw an e-mail from a social worker with the subject line "Tim's Mom." He didn't open it to read it, but he figured they were going over the legal deal about her.

Jamie went with her dad to Phoenix. Everyone would go for the final race in Florida. The Maxwells had a friend who owned a cottage on the beach, and they were going to stay there and celebrate Thanksgiving and the end of the racing season. When they discussed it, Tim said he needed to talk to his mom about Thanksgiving, which made Mrs. Maxwell turn away and work on the dishes.

After church on Sunday, Kellen went to a friend's house, and Tim sat in the living room to watch the prerace festivities. Mrs. Maxwell brought some popcorn and other stuff to munch on. He took a plate of veggies and dip and some stuffed mushrooms she had cooked and stood.

"Where are you headed?" she said.

"Out to the garage to watch the race," Tim said.

"You don't have to go out there. There's nobody coming over today."

"Why not?"

"I told them we wanted to watch alone. There's always a lot of activity around here."

Tim sat again and popped the top on a soda. “Think he’s gonna win?”

“I think he’ll be okay, no matter what happens. Which is what I think about you.”

Tim looked at her. She had lowered her voice and turned on the couch toward him. He put the plate down and sat back when she hit the Mute button.

“They’re about to have the flyover,” he said.

Her face was serious. “I have strong feelings about your mom and her asking you to come with her. But I can understand how you’d want to go with her. She’s your flesh and blood.”

He nodded. “She seemed pretty serious about it.”

Mrs. Maxwell didn’t say anything, and Tim imagined she wanted to say, *If she was so serious about it, why hasn’t she called you?*

“I’ve checked with the social worker and made some calls and sent some e-mails. If you want to go with your mom, we’ll understand. I’d be lying if I didn’t tell you I hope you’ll stay. I think it might be better to have your mom come visit or work out something like that. But if you want to go, we won’t stand in your way.”

He couldn’t believe it was that easy. He thought he’d have to sign a billion papers and promise never to come back or something. “Thanks.”

She hit the Mute button and they watched the

race. Kellen came back about midway through and ate just about everything Mrs. Maxwell had set out on the coffee table.

Though Tim was interested in the race, it was hard to concentrate. He wondered if something had happened to his mom. Or was she preparing a place where they could live? What would it be like to actually live with her?

His cell phone buzzed in his pocket, and he jumped up and ran to the next room to answer it.

"Hey, Tim," his mom said. "Sorry I didn't get a chance to call earlier. You doing okay?"

"Yeah, I'm fine. We're just watching the race at Phoenix."

"Oh, how's Maxwell doing?"

"He got a penalty for going too fast on pit road, so they sent him to the back, but he's making his way up."

"Good. Say, listen, is there any chance you'll be traveling with the family to Florida next week? I have an idea how we could meet up and start our new life."

Tim gulped. "They've been talking about this place they're going to stay down near Miami. But if you go back to Florida—"

"I'm going to get all that worked out. Don't worry. I just need to know if you're serious about coming with me. Are you?"

"Yeah, I've been thinking about it a lot. I just don't know how it would work."

"Leave that to me. Now, I'll call you before you get down there and get the address. Don't tell the Maxwells anything about this."

"Mom, I talked with Mrs. Maxwell, and she said—"

"I have to go. I'll see you in about a week, okay?"

"Yeah, okay. Bye." He hung up and thought about what she'd said.

Kellen gave a whoop from the other room, and Tim returned.

"Dad made it back into the top 20," Kellen said. "He's moving up."

Tim tried to focus on the race, but it was difficult. He wondered where he'd be staying next Sunday. Would his mom get a good job somewhere and have them move into an apartment—or even a house? Would they be on the road like he had been with his dad?

A crash marred the ending of the race, taking out half a dozen cars. Dale wasn't in the pile and he finished 11th—a good showing for all the trouble he had. The results flashed on the screen. The top four drivers were separated by only 10 points. Dale was in the fourth spot. He'd have to jump over three other drivers to win the championship.

"He's going to do it," Kellen said, hugging his mother.

She smiled, but Tim could tell something was bothering her. Something about him.

Chapter 38
Bungalow

JAMIE WANTED TO FLY down with her dad earlier in the week, but her mom said she'd missed enough school already, so the rest of the family arrived Saturday morning. The phone hadn't stopped ringing at the house with interview requests and people from the church wishing her dad well. The media played up the "little guy" angle about her dad, and it seemed like everyone in the country who wasn't rooting for the top three drivers was rooting for Dale Maxwell.

Of course, the fact that Butch Devalon was in the #1 spot didn't help quell the talk about the feud between Butch and her dad. Some made a big deal of the Tim angle, while others focused on the differences the two had on the track. The one that surprised her most was an article by Calvin Shoverton about a romance between Butch and her mom that Jamie had no idea about.

"We were young and I was foolish," her mom said. "I thought Butch was cute back then, but the few dates we had never went anywhere."

"Why not?"

Her mother gave her the look. "Because Butch liked to talk about his favorite subject all the time."

"Racing?" Jamie said.

"No. *Butch.* His favorite subject was himself and how many championships he was going to win and how much money he'd make. I wasn't a Christian back then, so I fell under his spell for a little while before reality came to me."

"Did you kiss him?" Jamie said, smiling.

Her mom rolled her eyes. "A couple of times, but your father is the only one I've truly kissed. Now can we change the subject?"

/////

The house near the beach was called a bungalow, which meant it was only one story, but it sprawled along the property. There was a private, in-ground pool in the back that was as big as the country club pool back in Velocity. Kellen's eyes widened when he saw it, and he ran into a room and changed into his bathing suit. He came running through the house, and seconds later they heard a splash.

Tim seemed preoccupied to Jamie, always fidgeting with his phone and not eating much. He jumped in the pool with Kellen with his T-shirt on. Later, when her dad came home and they went to the beach, Tim just walked along, looking at the water and kicking at the waves like a kid who'd never seen salt water before.

Jamie had never seen her dad so keyed up before a race. She talked with him about the points and different scenarios, but he always came back to, "We'll just have to see how it turns out."

The whole family (including Tim) was walking together when Jamie said, "I can tell you've got that calculator of a brain working up there. What'll it take to win the championship?"

Her dad smiled. "Well, let's say we all get the points we normally get for leading laps and such. It's complicated, but I pretty much have to finish several spots ahead of the other leaders."

"What about Butch?"

"I have to finish at least three spots ahead of him to beat him."

"So you're going to run it full tilt," Jamie said.

"What do I have to lose?" he said.

/////

Tim went to church with the Maxwells on Saturday evening at a big church with "Welcome NASCAR Fans" on the sign out front. The pastor had asked Dale to speak at the service. The family was led up front to a pew that was roped off for special guests.

The band played a couple of songs that had the people clapping and singing. Then the pastor got up and read a verse or two and introduced Dale. There was a lot of applause for him as he walked to the podium.

"When I was a kid," he said, "I dreamed about being in contention for the championship. When I actually became a driver, it was so real I could taste it. I've had some success over the years. I've lived the dream so many would love to live. But I'll tell you this: I wouldn't trade all the success I've had and even that trophy they're offering tomorrow for a second of knowing Jesus Christ as my Savior.

"Now that's a lot easier to say than it is to live. But to know that I have a relationship with the Creator, to know he has forgiven me, that I don't have to be afraid of what comes after this life, and that I can be excited about what's to come . . ."

Tim's cell buzzed, and he slipped to the side of the church and into the hallway.

"I'm here in Miami," his mother said. "Where are you?"

He told her.

"And where are you staying?"

He opened a piece of paper he had jammed into his pocket and read the address to her.

"Could you be ready to leave in the morning?"

"You mean before the race?" he said.

"Yeah, I want to get an early start. Can you be ready about nine?"

"Okay. I'll get my stuff together."

/////

The next morning, Tim was up with his suitcase by the door when Dale was ready to leave. He turned to Tim. "Your mom coming to get you?"

Tim nodded.

Dale stuck out a hand. "I can't tell you what a pleasure it's been to have you with us. You're like another son to me." He opened his wallet and pulled out a few bills.

"You don't have to do that," Tim said.

"I know. Take your mom out to dinner when you're on the road. If anything happens . . . well, just remember you have a place with us."

"I appreciate all you've done," Tim said, grabbing Dale's hand.

"And there's a spot for you on our team," Dale said. He stopped and looked like he wanted to say something else, then gave Tim a hug and walked out.

Later, when everyone else was ready to leave for the track, Mrs. Maxwell gave Tim a big hug and wiped away a tear. The water in her eyes brought a mist to his own.

"I knew this day would come," she said, "but I didn't think it would be this soon. I'll be praying for you every day."

"Thank you."

Jamie hugged him and Kellen stared. "I thought you were going to be my big brother. Forever."

"I will be," Tim said. "I'm just going to do it from a distance."

"Where?" Kellen said.

"I'm not sure. But I'll call and tell you. Maybe I can visit or something. We'll e-mail."

Kellen looked up at Tim. "I'm going to miss you." He hugged him, and Tim couldn't find any place to put his arms. He hadn't counted on feeling like this. Finally he put his arms around Kellen and gave him a hug he'd never forget.

"You're not coming to the race?" Jamie said to Tim.

"We could get your mom in if she wants," Mrs. Maxwell said.

"She wants to get on the road. I'll wait here for her if that's okay."

Mrs. Maxwell nodded. "Just lock the door when you leave. You have our phone numbers on your cell. Call us if anything goes wrong or if you need something."

Tim nodded. As the door was about to close, he reached out and stopped it. "Mrs. Maxwell, can you tell Dale something?"

"Sure. What is it?"

"Tell him to beat Devalon, okay?"

She smiled. "This race is for your dad."

Chapter 39
Homestead-Miami

JAMIE STOOD beside the car as her parents hugged and prayed. Her mom handed her dad a folded piece of paper, and Jamie moved closer to read it.

> *However, I consider my life worth nothing to me, if only I may finish the race and complete the task the Lord Jesus has given me—the task of testifying to the gospel of God's grace. (Acts 20:24, NIV)*

Her dad smiled. "That's it, darlin'. That's what this is all about, isn't it?"

Her mom said something, her face buried in his fire suit.

"I know," he said. "I miss him already too."

Her dad climbed into the car, and soon they lined up behind the pace car.

Jamie put on her headphones and caught sight of Chad Devalon three pit boxes away. He was laughing with one of the crew members, but when he turned and saw her, the smile faded.

Her dad had qualified in the seventh position to start the race, and he said it was the perfect number. When Jamie asked him to explain, he said, "Seven is the biblical number of completeness."

"I'd rather be number one," Jamie had said.

The first few laps were tentative for everyone. Though the top four drivers were in line for a possible championship, all 12 Chase drivers wanted to make moves, and the other 31 drivers wanted to finish the season well and end on a good note looking forward to Daytona in February. But no one wanted to be the person who knocked a potential champion out of the race.

"Butch Devalon moves forward two spots now and takes the lead on lap 12," the announcer said. "He's the favorite to win another championship, but there are a lot of guys behind him who want to stop him."

"Yeah, and one of those is in the #14 car there," a commentator said. "Dale Maxwell is looking for his first championship, and you can bet he knows exactly what he has to do in order to jump over the other contenders."

Jamie switched the radio to her dad's frequency. ". . . feels a little loose at the moment. I want to try an air pressure adjustment on the left side."

The #14 car was in fifth position, and the other two cars in contention for the cup, #11 and #76, were now in the middle of the field.

"Long race, Dale," T.J. said. "Don't push it here at the front."

"I want to lead a lap while I'm running well," her dad said.

He went on the outside around the three cars ahead of him and caught up to the #13 car. It looked like Devalon could feel him coming, and Jamie switched to the channel and heard Butch's voice.

"Yeah, I see him," Butch said.

"At your bumper," the spotter said.

"Not for long," Butch said.

With a burst of speed, #13 pulled ahead and her dad fell in behind him, following a car length away.

"That'll teach him," the spotter said.

"Got that right," Devalon said.

Jamie went back to her dad's channel and listened as he bided his time. When Devalon pitted under green, her dad stayed out and led a lap.

But two laps later, Scotty shouted into the microphone, "Stay low. Stay low. Come on. Come on! You're clear. . . . Good job."

"Think I picked up some debris back there," Dale said. "I'll need four tires when I come in."

His right front was nearly shredded when he slid into the pit stall. A jammed lug nut extended the pit stop, and when he returned to the track, he was in 15th place. Butch was just ahead of him in 11th place with cars #11 and #76 moving up to the third and fifth positions on the track. Both worked their way up to lead a lap, gaining precious points toward the championship.

"What would happen if we finished right now?" Kellen yelled over the noise.

"There'd be a lot of angry fans," Jamie said, chuckling.

"I can't watch," her mom said.

Jamie put an arm around her. "Finishing the race is not just for drivers, you know," she said, winking.

At lap 130, a rookie driver moved right, then came sharply down the track and collected the #11 car, sending him into the wall. The #11 driver climbed out, throwing his helmet onto the pavement. Everybody in the pit area said, "Ooooh," knowing how much helmets cost. Though Jamie was glad to have one person out of contention, she felt bad for both drivers, especially the rookie who got out of his car and almost crawled back to the garage.

Butch Devalon moved back into the top 10, and her dad remained farther back, staying between the

15th and 20th positions. It was a strategy he'd used before—conserving his engine and tires and waiting to pounce. The only question was whether he had enough time to make it work.

One of the seven caution flags came out on lap 249, and the leaders came in for tires and fuel.

"You should be good for the rest of the way, Dale," T.J. said.

"Ten-four."

The #14 car exited pit road in the 12th position. On a single-file restart, her dad shot low and went around two cars that were slow to the line. One of them was the #76. Jamie about jumped out of her skin when she saw that.

Butch Devalon had made his way back to first place and seemed to be pulling away from the field—not a good sign for the Maxwell crew. The only glimmer of hope was that her dad was matching his lap speeds almost exactly.

"He'll slow down in a few laps," T.J. said, and Jamie could hear the wishful thinking in his voice.

By lap 257, the #14 car had closed the gap and was racing in third place. The #76 car had backed off into the 20s.

"Looks like it's Butch vs. Dale now," the commentator said. "And if they finish one and two, Butch is going to take the cup again."

"Ten laps to go to see who will win the cup—"

"And Dale's in the second position now, about five car lengths behind Butch. They've both run clean out here today, and it looks like they're only getting stronger."

Her dad closed the gap to two car lengths on the next lap. With six laps to go he was at Devalon's rear end.

"If Dale steals the air from him, he could spin Butch out," the commentator said. "If it were the other way around, Dale leading, I'd bet Butch would do that, but I don't think Dale will. Look at that—he's moving down on the inside."

Her dad's car was at the door of #13 and pulling even into turn one. He accelerated into the turn, trading paint with #13 as he went a little high. The rest of the field had fallen back, and Devalon and Maxwell were passing lapped traffic. Her dad pulled half a car length ahead. In turn four, he cleared Devalon and #13 got behind #14.

"Watch and see if Butch tries to get him loose in one of these turns," the commentator said. "Five laps to go."

"Butch should just back off here," the announcer said. "He's the cup champion as it stands. The last thing he should want to do is chance a crash."

"You don't tell a guy like Butch to back off," the

commentator said. "He wants to win this race. That's in his blood."

Her dad held a slim lead, and the rest of the pack fell back. It was #14 in front of #13 as they came down the back straightaway.

The crowd stood and cheered as the engines roared, and Jamie got a little misty-eyed. If things stayed the way they were now, her dad would win, but he'd be in second place in the Chase. "We need some help," she said to Kellen.

"Want me to run onto the track and throw a shoe at Devalon's windshield?"

Jamie shook her head and smiled. "There's nobody close enough to block him or get in front of him." She looked at the sky, darkening now. Did God care about the outcome of NASCAR races? Did he care who came in first, last, or was the lucky dog?

"Four laps to go as Dale Maxwell tries to hold off Butch Devalon for the win here at Homestead," the announcer said. "And unless something drastic happens, Butch is going to be the cup—"

"Look at this coming up behind them," the commentator said. "The #76 car got a burst of speed, and he's closing the gap on the leaders."

They were on the backstretch when #76 pulled behind Devalon to make it three cars, single file. In turn four all three cars were within inches of each other.

"Oh, look out!" the commentator said. "Dale got loose out of turn four, and he did a good job of hanging on. But here comes—"

"*Oh!* Devalon went low on the apron, and it looked like he overcorrected."

"Yeah, he did."

"The #13 and #76 hit hard, and it looks like they both got into Dale a bit too, but he was able to hold on to it. The caution is out."

"I would not want to be down there when Butch climbs out of that car."

"We're getting word that we'll have one more try to complete this race when the debris is cleared from the track."

Jamie watched in stunned silence. Devalon's car wasn't as badly damaged as the #76, and with four tires, he was able to come back onto the track, though way behind the leaders.

On the restart, her dad shot forward, and it almost looked like the field was giving him the championship.

"White flag, white flag," a spotter said.

With tears in her eyes, Jamie watched her dad sail through the final lap, as if he were riding on a cloud. Butch Devalon limped home in 33rd place while her dad took the checkered flag. Jamie glanced at Kellen, then her mom, her mouth in an O.

"Hot dog, Dale did it!" the commentator said.

"And if my calculations are correct, Dale wins by the slimmest of margins, only one point over Butch Devalon."

"Can you believe that? I'll tell you what. This is the kind of racing the fans love to see, fighting and gouging right to the end. I hate to see Butch lose—he's getting out of his car now, and he doesn't look too happy."

"Well, he only has himself to blame because he could have backed off and won the cup if he hadn't pushed it. Here's the replay now. . . ."

Chapter 40
Winner's Circle

JAMIE JOINED her dad, the rest of the family, and the crew in the winner's circle. Soda was in the air, and she couldn't hold back the smiles. Her dad was interviewed as soon as he jumped onto the ground, and he was all smiles as well.

"I want to pay tribute to Butch in the #13 and Rusty in #76," her dad said. "They were fine competitors out there, and I just managed to squeak by. And the #11 car could have been right here too if it hadn't had a tough break. But I want to thank our sponsors and the crew and everybody back at the garage in Velocity. I'm proud to be standing here today and a giving testimony to God's grace. My wife gave me a verse before I started today, and I'll end it by thanking God for giving me the privilege of winning this. It's only by his strength that I can do anything."

The reporter pulled the microphone back and asked about the wreck.

Her dad said that as soon as Butch got into him, he floored it and tried to punch through. "I got smacked in the left rear, and the car was a little hard to handle on the last couple of laps, but I wasn't about to let it get away from me."

"How's it feel to be the new cup champion?" the reporter said.

"Well, it's a lifelong dream come true." He looked at Jamie's mom. "And this is probably as good a time as any to announce something I've been thinking about for a long time. There's going to be another bay in our garage because I'm taking on a new driver next year." He put his arm around Jamie. "She helped me get to this point, and I'm hoping we get to race together in the next few years."

"What do you think about that, Jamie?" the reporter said.

Jamie grinned. "It's kind of hard to believe. I guess I should wait to see if there are any better offers, but okay. You're on, Dad."

The two embraced, and Kellen and her mom jumped into the pile, along with T.J., Scotty, and the rest of the crew.

"David beats Goliath," the announcer said.

"Yeah, and David's daughter might just be better than her dad," the commentator said.

Chapter 41
News

JAMIE HEARD the phone ring the next morning and rolled over in bed to go back to sleep. It was her dad's "What!?" that got her up. She ran into the kitchen, where her mom sat with an open Bible. Her dad's Bible was in his place, and he was pacing the kitchen.

"You've got to be kidding me," her dad said.

"Is it about Tim?" Jamie said.

Her mother shrugged. "I don't know."

Kellen came out, rubbing his eyes and yawning. "What's all the shouting for?"

"So there's nothing we can do? What about an appeal?"

"Maybe it's about Tim's mom," Jamie whispered.

Her dad walked into the bedroom. When he came out he was shaking his head. He plopped into his chair like a dead fish.

"What?" the three of them said in unison.

"The car failed a postrace inspection," he said. "We were too low on the left rear."

"It was the accident!" Jamie said. "Devalon slammed into you, and it mashed the back end down. How can you control that?"

"They can't take the win from you, can they?" Kellen said.

"Not the win," he said. "But they're taking the cup away."

There was silence for a split second, then a trio of angry voices.

"That's not fair!"

"They can't do that!"

"You didn't do anything wrong, Dad!"

"There has to be something you can do—file a protest or something. Write the president!"

When everyone had quieted, Jamie put her head in her hands and groaned. "Oh no, you know what this means, don't you?"

"What?" Kellen said.

"Devalon gets the cup. Butch Devalon is going to win on a technicality."

Her mom stood and rubbed her dad's back. "I can't imagine how you must feel."

He took a deep breath and blew it out. "Well, at least I won't have the pressure of defending my title next year.

T.J. said there was a bad weld in one of the shocks. At least we didn't get the penalty because we cheated."

Jamie shook her head. "All that publicity, all those interviews for winning—I thought that was part of God's plan. That you'd get to be up in front of all those people and get to tell them about God."

He nodded. "That's what I thought, but I guess it wasn't meant to be." Her dad sat and flipped through his Bible. Then he got up and poured Kellen a bowl of cereal. He paced through the kitchen, running a hand through his hair.

Jamie still couldn't believe the turn of events. She felt numb.

Finally her dad said, "I think I'll take a walk on the beach."

"You want me to go with you?" her mom said.

"I think I need to be by myself for a little bit."

When her dad had gone, Jamie and her mom just listened to Kellen crunch his cereal. Then he slurped his milk. Then he banged the spoon on the side of the bowl.

"Would you stop that!" Jamie snapped.

"What did I do?" Kellen said. He put his bowl in the sink.

All three of them sighed at the same time.

"I miss Tim," Kellen said. "Can I call him, Mom?"

"No. Not yet. Let's give him some time."

"I just want to see how he is."

"Wonder if he heard about the race," Jamie said.

Her mom did the breakfast dishes. When Kellen started to turn on the TV, she stopped him. "We've had enough coverage of your dad. Let's leave it."

Jamie wanted to go home, but her dad insisted they take advantage of the beach house. On Tuesday they drove a short way to Everglades National Park. They rented four bikes and rode the extensive trails. Jamie liked the Long Pine Key ride, where they saw a few alligators sleeping along the sides of the path. At one point her dad got a little close, and a gator lunged at him.

By Wednesday they were feeling better about the loss of the cup, though the sting was still there for all of them. Jamie's dad did a couple of interviews near the track about the season and the loss. Jamie watched the report late in the day and had to switch it off when she saw Butch Devalon's face.

After her mom had prepared the turkey for cooking the next day, they played Scrabble with girls against the boys. Kellen kept playing words like *it* and *to*, and her dad couldn't quit laughing. Jamie and her mom won going away.

/////

Jamie went for a walk on the deserted beach the next morning. She liked looking for shells and digging her feet in the wet sand. She found herself praying, just talking to God as she walked along. She prayed for the people she knew who weren't Christians—Vanessa came to her mind and Tim, of course. She also prayed for Cassie and some others in her youth group.

She stopped and looked out at the vastness of the ocean. A smile came to her face. "This is totally not what I expected to be doing," she said out loud. "If you'd have asked me six months ago if I'd be walking on the beach, praying to you, and enjoying it, I wouldn't have believed it. I think that's what I'm most thankful for this year."

When she got home, she helped her mom in the kitchen, making some stuffing. Her dad always made a fruit salad with cranberry sauce that everybody loved and cut the turkey. Kellen played a new NASCAR video game, and instead of racing to win, he spent a half hour smashing into the #13 car. Her dad laughed at him.

Kellen set the table as Jamie and her parents brought the food in. It was enough for a small army, like each Thanksgiving. Jamie's mom looked at a fifth plate at the end of the table and Kellen frowned. "Sorry. I just got in the habit of setting five places instead of four."

They joined hands, and her dad cleared his throat. "Father, we want to thank you for the things you've brought into our lives this past year. For the successes and the failures. For the decisions you guided us through. For our family. And we think about the one missing from us. . . ." His voice caught and Jamie glanced over. Her dad had his chin down, tight against his chest.

"You love Tim even more than we do," her mom prayed, picking it up from Jamie's dad. "We thank you for what you taught us through him. We ask you to draw him and his mom to yourself. We give him to you. . . ."

There was an awkward pause again, and Jamie saw her mom bring her napkin to her eyes.

The next voice she heard was Kellen's. "Lord, Tim's had a lot of tough breaks. I just think he needs to be with us. So I pray you'd bring him back somehow."

"Amen," Jamie said.

"Amen," everybody else said.

Jamie started with stuffing, turkey, and mashed potatoes, along with some of the fruit salad. She put butter on her roll and was about to dig in when someone tapped at the front door. They all looked at each other.

"Who could that be?" her mom said.

Kellen was the first up and to the door. When he opened it, Jamie gasped.

"Man, that prayer really worked!" Kellen said. "And fast!"

"Tim!" Jamie said.

He had his suitcase with him on the sidewalk, and he looked exhausted. "I was hoping you guys would still be here."

"Where's your mom?" Jamie said.

Tim put his suitcase down on the front step as Kellen dragged him inside. "Well, that's kind of a long story. But to be honest, I don't think it's going to work for me to stay with her. At least not for now." Kellen had Tim in the kitchen now, and Tim glanced at the food on the table. He looked as hungry as a wolf. "I was kind of thinking that if your offer was still good . . . I mean, I'll understand if you don't want to, but—"

Jamie's dad took Tim's suitcase and gave him a bear hug. "Welcome home, Tim. And happy Thanksgiving."

"Get washed up and join us," Jamie's mom said. "We already set you a place at the table."

"Really?" Tim said, taking a look at the empty plate.

Tears came to Jamie's eyes. She wasn't sure why. Maybe she'd never understand what it was about Tim that touched her deep inside. But her dad had said it all in that one word.

Home.

Afterword

You now know one slice of the history of that year, finishing as one of the most exciting in the Chase and one of the most controversial. After Dale's championship was taken away—something that caused an uproar inside and outside the world of NASCAR—the rules committee changed the way they dealt with accidental infractions. Fans applauded the change, but it wasn't until years later that Dale was given a special award by NASCAR for that year.

That was also the year Jamie took a huge step toward her own racing career. I won't spoil the rest of her story, but suffice it to say that she made a huge impact on the sport.

Perhaps even more interesting is the series of twists and turns, highs and lows, victories and tragedies of Tim Carhardt. I'm proud to say that I met both Tim and Jamie when they were young, when few people knew their names.

Of course, all of racing had to deal with the Devalon dynasty, but Dale Maxwell took advantage of the controversy by publishing a book about the season, his life, and his faith. Some said he got more publicity for having the championship taken away, and therefore he reached more people with his message. (That *was* a book I was privileged to help Dale write.)

Many will wonder what happened to Kellen in the years following and if Cassie Strower ever got to realize her dream of serving in overseas missions. Jenna, the young girl Jamie met at Camp Left Turn, became a good friend of the Maxwell family, along with many of the kids at the camp who became avid fans of Dale and Jamie.

I've learned a lot from the Maxwells. I've learned God can do much through people who let him work through them. And that winning isn't always the most important thing in racing or in life.

It's a good lesson for all of us.

Calvin Shoverton,
Motorsports Senior Reporter, *Charlotte Times*

Acknowledgments

Brian and Jan, thanks for your enthusiasm about this series. Special thanks to David Alford of Turtle Wax and the Paul Menard team—you answered all my questions and then some. Ron Dabisch of the Richard Petty Driving Experience—thanks for letting me go 134.29 and not get a ticket. Also thanks to Gina Mooi and Coleman Pressley, two up-and-coming drivers. I hope to see you both racing for the cup one day on the same track. Also, Doug Hastings of Moody Broadcasting and Brookside Motorsports for sending updates and providing ideas, though you didn't always know it. Thanks to Shawn and Sean Matthuis of Brookside Motorsports, the father and son team on the #0 Kids Corner car. And to Roger Basick of WMBI, Chicago.

About the Author

CHRIS FABRY is a writer, broadcaster, and graduate of Richard Petty Driving Experience (top speed: 134.29 mph). He has written more than 50 books, including collaboration on the Left Behind: The Kids, Red Rock Mysteries, and The Wormling series.

You may have heard his voice on Focus on the Family, Moody Broadcasting, or Love Worth Finding. He has also written for *Adventures in Odyssey*, *Radio Theatre*, and *Kids Corner*.

Chris is a graduate of the W. Page Pitt School of Journalism at Marshall University in Huntington, West Virginia. He and his wife, Andrea, have nine children and live in Colorado.

If you'd like to get in touch with the author, you can reach him at chrisfabry@comcast.net.

RED ROCK MYSTERIES

#1 Haunted Waters

#2 Stolen Secrets

#3 Missing Pieces

#4 Wild Rescue

#5 Grave Shadows

#6 Phantom Writer

#7 Double Fault

#8 Canyon Echoes

#9 Instant Menace

#10 Escaping Darkness

#11 Windy City Danger

#12 Hollywood Holdup

#13 Hidden Riches

#14 Wind Chill

#15 Dead End

BRYCE AND ASHLEY TIMBERLINE are normal 13-year-old twins, except for one thing—they discover action-packed mystery wherever they go. Wanting to get to the bottom of any mystery, these twins find themselves on a nonstop search for truth.

CP0140